In The Garden Air

Patsy Collins

Copyright © 2022 Patsy Collins

All rights reserved.
The stories in this book are subject to copyright.
They may not be copied or transmitted in any way
without the permission of the copyright holder,
except for brief quotes used in reviews.

These stories are works of fiction.

The author can be found at
www.patsycollins.uk

ISBN-978-1-914339-26-4

In memory of my much loved and much missed gardening grandparents; Anthea, Cyril, and Daisy.

Contents

1. Making Cuts..1
2. Hello Again...5
3. Kenny Fears The Worst...10
4. Daisy Chains...13
5. Bath Night...25
6. Saying It With Flowers..32
7. Valentine's Gimmick..36
8. On A Summer Day...43
9. Roundabout Rose..44
10. Holiday Temptations..47
11. A Little Less Self Restraint.......................................51
12. The Perfect Line...55
13. Faraway Friends..62
14. Shopping Lists..68
15. Awkward Arrangement..74
16. Lily Of The Valley...81
17. A Little Rain Must Fall..85
18. Breaking With Routine...91
19. In The Pink...95
20. All About Her...103
21. Part Of The Place...118
22. A Year In A Garden...123
23. A Year In The New Garden.....................................132
24. Not Disappointing The Kids....................................145

1. Making Cuts

Dorothy hears the distant sound of a lawnmower and smiles. The sound will grow increasingly loud as one by one, each of her neighbour's lawnmowers is started up and their little patches of grass cut tidily short. At one time she'd hated the noise as it came towards her in a kind of horticultural Mexican sound wave.

A few years ago she'd regularly have her clean washing smothered in debris as the council came by, cutting down all the lovely wild flowers on the verge opposite her house. Everyone seemed equally annoyed. Motorists got cross because the huge mowers held up traffic. Nature lovers were saddened as the cuts seemed to come just as the flowers were about to bloom and feed the insects. Council tax payers were incensed their money wasn't being put to better use. Anyone living close by was irritated by the dust and noise.

Then cuts of a different kind came. Whether you blamed the current government or the last one, the facts were the same; there wasn't enough money to pay for regular verge trimming. Although sympathetic to those who'd lost jobs and concerned what those financial cuts would mean to youngsters like her grandson Luke, Dorothy was pleased the grass and flowers were left to grow.

Her neighbours had, of course, continued to cut their lawns. She'd hear the annoying noise for a while, then it seemed to stop. In reality the gardener was moving his mower from front garden to back, or vice versa, and the noise soon started up again. Why people bothered with grass in the tiny space out the front Dorothy didn't know. She'd replaced hers with rose and lavender bushes. Caring for them was easier than lugging the mower down the side path and in summer they provided colour and scent.

Just as she was sure whoever it was really had finished another mower would start. She supposed seeing or hearing the first person prompted neighbours to remark, "Everyone is doing their grass, we'd better do ours," or, "Seems Bill thinks it will stay dry long enough to mow the lawn, he's usually right about the weather." So on and on it went all day.

The noise wasn't really the trouble. From indoors it was just an irritation which made it a little difficult to hear the television or concentrate on her book. It was only fairly recently the mowing had truly bothered her. Dorothy found it increasingly difficult and tiring to manage her mower and therefore only did it when absolutely necessary. Her neighbour Bill was of a similar age. He tired easily, like her. On the days he cut the grass he soon went back inside rather than stop out weeding or pruning; tasks which allowed him to chat to Dorothy over the fence as they worked.

It wasn't just selfishness and a hunger for conversation which made Dorothy dread the sound of the mowers. Bill, although still accurate in his weather predictions, was no longer perfectly steady on his feet. Dorothy worried manoeuvring the mower from shed to back garden and then from back to front would result in his having a fall. She'd never said as much, but Bill meant more to her than just another friendly neighbour.

On mowing days, instead of shutting herself inside where she couldn't hear the noise, she'd taken to opening the windows and keeping an anxious watch. She was doing that as Luke arrived. When Bill opened his gate, her grandson jumped over Dorothy's lavender hedge to help him.

"Thanks, lad," Bill wheezed as Luke set the mower down for him.

Dorothy thanked him too. "And thank you for stopping by. I know you're busy job hunting."

"I was. Pretty much given up now. All the cuts mean there aren't many jobs about and as I've got no experience and no references I don't have a chance of even getting an interview."

Bill, who was still catching his breath, clearly overheard this. "It's not much of a job, but if you're at a loose end I'd happily give you a few quid to mow my grass. If you do it regular I could write a reference. That might help."

It didn't take Luke long to tidy up Bill's front lawn and negotiate a small fee for doing the whole garden each week. Once the neighbours saw Luke did a good job, and heard his rates, he was asked to cut theirs too. Then people asked him if he could trim back a hedge, dig over a flower bed, or clear out a pond. Between them Bill or Dorothy were able to give Luke the instructions he needed to complete the jobs.

"You're a fast learner, lad," Bill said. "Why not try this?" He gave Luke a page from the newspaper advertising a part time college course in garden maintenance.

Luke signed up and as his knowledge increased, so did his workload. He never did need that reference from Bill, not even to secure a loan for the van which enabled him to reach customers further away and expand his part time job into a full time business. It spread like a horticultural Mexican wave.

"It's you who got him started," Dorothy told Bill. "Thank you for that."

"Yeah well, the lad's important to you." Bill's face flushed and he turned his attention back to his own side of the fence.

"You could come round for a cuppa when you've finished, if you like."

Now Dorothy loves the sound of the first lawnmower on a Tuesday morning. It's her signal to start baking the lemon drizzle cake Luke loves, so it's just cool enough to cut when he reaches her house for his lunch break. Afterwards he mows her lawn. Then the sound of the mower grows fainter and fainter as he works his way down the road.

It's soon quiet enough again for her to chat to Bill over another cup of tea and the last of the cake.

2. Hello Again

The invitation to Joy's wedding was a surprise. We'd been good friends at school, but drifted apart. We sent Christmas cards and kept in touch through Facebook, and I suppose a wedding is the time when you want to believe happy relationships last forever.

It took me a while to decide whether or not to accept. So long in fact that Joy had to prompt me. It wasn't because of her. Joy is a nice person, pretty much lives up to her name in fact. It wasn't that the invitation was for a wedding either. Despite never being married myself, I'm not against the whole thing. There was someone I'd have liked to marry, but it didn't happen.

The reason for my reluctance was Joy's future husband. Not him precisely, but the fact that he was friends with Tomas back when I used to hang out with Joy. If she was looking up old friends and inviting them, wasn't it likely her fiancé would too? I couldn't very well ask if Tomas would be there. "Hey, Joy, about that chap I was engaged to one summer and pretend I hardly remember? Is he going to be a guest? Because if so my heart will break all over again."

Tomas apart, it promised to be a good wedding. Joy was an only child and her parents well off. The venue was famed for its superb gardens and fabulous food. I'd share a happy occasion and meet up with old friends. It was the gardens, a fact which finally persuaded me. I've visited each time they've opened to the public and absolutely loved it, but such opportunities are rare. The property is still owned by the family who live in part of it and lease out the rest for weddings, corporate functions and as a backdrop for films.

For the ceremony I'd sit with 'friends of the bride'. Tomas, if he was there, would be on the groom's side. I could ask Joy to sit me with some of our other school friends for the reception. No need to mention not wanting to be right next to anyone else.

Once I'd decided to go, I started to look forward to it. First off Joy invited me to the hen-night. I accepted; it seemed like a good idea. Then she suggested those of us who'd been friends in our teens meet up for a pre hen-night bash. That seemed an excellent idea. I'd meet most of the people who'd be likely to remember me and therefore notice the change.

Should I warn anyone was my next dilemma. I didn't want to make a big announcement. Thanks to social media I didn't have to. All I did was change the head only profile picture for one of me in my latest wheelchair and comment how the new wheels allowed me greater independence than I'd known since my early twenties.

I was quite proud of the way I handled it, upbeat and cheerful. Making it clear it was nothing new, so no one felt awkward or had to sympathise. As expected word got round and by the time I met up with the girls no one looked surprised I'd brought my own seat. Instead of shock that I could literally no longer stand on my legs there was admiration for the way I metaphorically stood on my own two feet by living alone, holding down a job and driving an adapted car.

They didn't need to know how long it took me to learn to do those things, how long it had taken to care enough about myself to try. They didn't have to know my managing alone wasn't so much admirable as selfish. I allowed no one close to me to help. My foster parents wanted to, but I didn't let them give up their home and lives for a child who, just as she should have been off their hands, was set to be an even greater burden.

I'm not being fair to them. Of course they've helped me. I refused to stay living with them in the home they offered to have converted, but they still made changes so I can easily visit, even stay overnight. They didn't give up their jobs to care for me, but every day off was spent taking me to hospital, or visiting me or decorating my flat. They still help hugely and never seem to resent it. Perhaps they would have begun to if I'd been a greater burden still, but I'm pleased I didn't have to learn that.

The pre hen-night event was lots of fun. I hadn't expected that. Getting through it without upsetting anyone, myself included, had been the aim. There were tears, but all of them from laughter. I was well accustomed to aches and other bodily discomforts but had forgotten a person's ribs really could feel sore from laughing and their face grow stiff from a continuous beaming grin. I made a mental note to tell my physiotherapist about that. She'd find it amusing I was sure.

I thought I might be useful. I don't drink and there's room for four passengers in my car. I don't dance so I'm convenient for minding drinks and handbags. Some of the girls accepted a lift home, but they didn't accept non working legs as an excuse to avoid the dance floor. They insisted I join them and requested song after song which could be sort of danced to with a variety of arm movements.

I wasn't a good dancer, but I'd long since learned you don't need to be good to enjoy doing something. I'm not much good at the gardening, yet I help with around the grounds of the flats where I live. It gives me huge pleasure to see flowers which were once seeds I'd sprinkled onto the earth. Someone else had to dig it first, but I chose the golden yellow Californian poppies, the burgundy red nasturtiums and the burnt orange calendulas. With special long handled tools I removed some of the weeds and thinned the seedlings so they grew strongly and I watered them when they needed it. Thankfully that need only arose in warm weather as I ended up as damp as my beloved plants.

Joy's hen-night was fun too. Not quite such a carefree reversion to our schoolgirl selves as the previous event, because members of Joy and her fiancé's family joined us as well as her work colleagues. There was more eating, less drinking and no dancing. The laughter was more restrained to start with, the chatter would have made more sense to anyone who overheard than was the case with the first event, but we all had a good time.

The wedding service was beautiful and moving. Joy herself looked wonderful and not a person there could have doubted she was well named. I sat with friends – no longer friends from the past, but women who were current friends and whom I'd laugh with in the future. People who after a hasty apology on my part for pushing them away and regret on theirs for allowing it, had all agreed we'd keep our reminiscences to the stuff that filled our throats not with uncomfortable lumps but with giggling laughter.

Tomas was there. Thankfully I'd learned beforehand that he would be, so it wasn't a shock. Maybe it wouldn't have been anyway. Even when I told him I never wanted to see him again I knew I probably would. That had been a long time ago; three days after he told me he wasn't going back for his second term at university. I needed him, he said.

I didn't say anything right away. I couldn't. I said a lot in the next few days. That he wanted me to feel indebted to him, to make me feel trapped into staying with him. I claimed he was using me as an excuse not to work hard, that he was scared he'd fail in his dream to become a surgeon. That I'd wanted to dump him for some time but put up with him for fear of wrecking his career. He'd taken a lot of convincing and I'd had to say truly awful things, but eventually he'd gone back to university and directed his hurt into his studies. I knew he was more than hurt; broken, desolate, defeated. I knew because he'd loved me as much as I loved him and I too was broken, desolate and defeated.

Not now though. He's qualified, married, a father. He's happy and it shows on his face as he walks through the sumptuous flower borders towards me.

My life is different, of course it is, but after some difficult years I've learned I have a life worth living. I have a job which I do pretty well. I have friends and the man who digs the garden before I sprinkle seeds has hinted he'd like more of a relationship. Perhaps I'm ready to give that a try. First though I have to smile at Tomas, to congratulate him on his success and tactfully steer the conversation away from the past. I must say hello and never for a moment show that saying goodbye was the hardest thing I ever had to do.

3. Kenny Fears The Worst

Kenny unpacked, hoping he hadn't forgotten anything important. Mum and Dad weren't going to kill him until Saturday morning, but he didn't want to risk going home that Friday afternoon.

Good, the torch was there so he could read his comics. It was a shame he'd miss watching Crackerjack, but The Beano might take his mind off his worries. If not 2000 AD definitely would. He could read it and imagine what it would be like in the future when it really was 2000 AD and he was as old as Dad and nothing bad could happen to him. He counted up. He'd be nearly thirty-six! That might be even older than Dad. He definitely wouldn't have to go to school then, or do jobs, or be killed so his sister Maggie could go on holiday.

Kenny had a big bottle of Cherryade to drink and plenty of food. Lots of crisps and sweets, a Battenburg cake, butterscotch Angel Delight and a bottle of milk to make it with. He also had apple pies and a tomato because Mum said fruit and vegetables would keep him healthy and he didn't want to be ill before Granny and Granddad came. Kenny really missed them. They used to live down the road, but since they went to live in Ireland he'd only seen them three times and that was in nearly a year! They would be coming to stay again on Wednesday which was days and days away. Even so it didn't seem fair that Mum and Dad couldn't wait until then to take Maggie on holiday. If they did, Granny and

Granddad could look after him and he wouldn't have to be killed.

He'd hoped he had made a mistake like when Mum and Dad told him about Maggie. He thought they were going to get a baby instead of him, but they explained she would be his sister and they'd still love him just as much. At first they did, but now they made him do writing and adding up every single night for hours and hours. They said it was to get him ready to go back to school in a few week's time.

Granny and Granddad never made him go to school. Kenny went to their house the last time he thought he would be killed. He'd been playing in the garden and accidentally kicked his football into Mr Boyd's greenhouse and Mr Boyd shouted he would kill Kenny. Kenny ran away to Granny and Granddad's until Mum and Dad came to say it was safe to go home. They told him that sometimes people said things they didn't mean when they were angry. Mr Boyd was very angry with Kenny, but he wasn't really going to kill him.

This time it was different. Mum and Dad weren't angry. They had been happy they were going to kill him. They said they wouldn't tell him, it would be a surprise. They didn't tell him about Granny and Granddad coming either, but he supposed that was because they thought he would be dead and would miss it.

He tried to get comfortable while he waited for Wednesday and Granny and Granddad. Luckily he'd chosen a really good place to run away to. There was a bed and quilt and pillows. The lights wouldn't go on, but that was OK because he had his torch.

After his tea, Kenny read until he thought it must be bed time and then tried to go to sleep. Then he heard footsteps and there was a knock on the door!

"Kenny love, you can't live in the caravan. For one thing, it won't be staying in the garden; we need it tomorrow," Mum said. "If you really want to run away, you'll have to live somewhere else."

"Aren't you going to kill me?" he asked.

"No." She let herself in. "We were hoping to take you to Ireland with us to see Granny and Granddad."

"But they're coming to see us on Wednesday," he pointed out. "I heard you say that when you said you were going to kill me."

Mum started to laugh, then she said sorry and hugged him. "You poor love! You must have overheard us say we're going to Kilkenny. That's the name of the place in Ireland where Granny and Granddad live. We're setting off tomorrow, but won't reach them until Wednesday."

4. Daisy Chains

Angus probably wouldn't ever have felt ready to leave hospital if they hadn't changed the privacy curtains around the beds. The ones he'd seen when he first came round from surgery were a bit faded and dingy looking, but had restful images of boats. The bright new ones probably seemed more cheerful to most people, but to Angus the pattern of white and yellow daisies felt like an accusation.

The car crash which killed his girlfriend and caused serious injuries to Angus, keeping him confined to the ward for weeks, hadn't been his fault. On one level he knew that. He even had vague recollections of the other vehicle approaching way too fast, of there being nowhere to go on the narrow country lane and him desperately applying the brakes. Even after learning the other driver had been on the phone, Angus blamed himself for taking Daisy out that night.

"Come and stay with us," his brother, Donald, had urged, when the doctors decided he was ready for discharge.

At first he'd refused. "You've got enough to do without bothering about me."

"We've got enough to do without driving into town and battling for a parking space every day, so we can visit you."

"Do come," his sister-in-law added. "The girls miss their Uncle Angus."

His nieces visited twice a week, but he knew what she

meant. Angus was no longer the person he used to be. He knew he had to do something and the bright, daisy-patterned curtains gave him the final push to move on at least physically.

Living with Donald was supposed to be a temporary arrangement until he could cope on his own. Angus knew he should be able to do that now, but it seemed wrong for him to be getting on with his life when his beloved Daisy was gone.

The house was too crowded with Angus in what should have been one of the girl's rooms. He tried not to intrude too much and went out for walks, partly as physiotherapy, building up the strength in his legs, and partly to give them space.

Physically he recovered well and could walk fairly long distances without pain and had hardly a trace of a limp. He took little interest in his surroundings until one day he almost tripped on a purse on the ground. A young family had just come out of the nearby café and were walking away. Probably one of them had dropped it.

Angus wasn't up to running at the best of times and when he turned the purse over and saw the big leather daisy stitched on the front, he wasn't at his best. Instead of the cut out petals, he saw Daisy's freckled face grinning at him and saying, "About time too," when he'd eventually plucked up the courage to ask her out. Now it was too late to tell her again that he loved her. When he came to his senses the family were out of sight.

Angus checked the purse to see if there was a bank card or ID. Instead he found a few coins, a packet of sweets, several tiny pebbles and shells, a hair slide with an enormous and presumably fake jewel, and three tiny, plastic fairies. No doubt they were all some small girl's treasure. He knew how much his nieces valued pretty trinkets of sentimental value; the ribbons they'd had in their hair when they'd been bridesmaids, ornaments he'd won them at the fair before the crash, things their friends had given them. The loss of this purse would be a mini tragedy to whoever it belonged to. He had to return it.

The café the family had come out of was closed by then, so he took the purse home in the hope that his nieces would recognise it. They didn't but confirmed his belief that it was important to return it to the owner.

Unusually for him, Angus got up before nine the next day and was at the café before it opened.

The café owner thought the purse seemed familiar. "There's a family of regulars and one of the kids is often playing with little fairies she keeps in a purse like that," she said.

Angus showed her the contents.

"That's them, definitely. I don't know the name, but they come in every Wednesday at about five."

"Will you give this back to them?"

"It might get lost here. You walk by most days, why not give it to them yourself?"

Angus was so surprised she'd noticed him that he agreed.

"I'm not really open yet, but if you'll keep an eye on things for me while I fetch a few supplies from my van, you can have a cuppa on the house."

Angus made himself useful holding open the door when she brought in the first box and then fetching the rest for her. He was rewarded with a Danish pastry as well as a drink. He was the only person there until he'd almost finished, and the owner chatted as she bustled about getting the café ready for the day's trade. A dark haired girl walked in just as he was leaving and they exchanged tentative smiles as he held open the door for her.

When he returned to Donald's home, Angus saw the kitchen was in chaos. Was it always like that after the rush to get everyone fed and off to work and school? He'd been fairly oblivious to his surroundings for some time, but felt sure there wasn't usually so much mess. Probably it was his fault for being in the way that morning. Angus made up for it by doing the washing up and cleaning the kitchen floor. He did a thorough job, taking the bins out of the way and emptying them before returning them to the clean floor once it was dry.

With his face so close to the skirting board, he couldn't help noticing the paintwork there and around the door frame was beginning to peel. Donald and his wife had repeatedly said to make himself at home, so Angus found sandpaper, paint brushes and everything else he needed to prepare the woodwork and apply undercoat.

Although embarrassed by his brother and sister-in-law's thanks, Angus continued working on their house. It felt so good to do something useful for a change and to concentrate on something other than his guilt and grief. He even began to sleep right through the night.

On the Wednesday he returned the purse to the grateful owner.

"Please let me buy you a drink and cake to say thank you," the mother offered.

He'd have refused if she'd let him, but seeing that wasn't going to be an option, he'd accepted tea and a doughnut. It was delicious. Angus wished he had money to buy some for his nieces and their parents, but he'd insisted on having all his benefits paid into their account, to help towards his keep.

Angus fell into a pattern of rising early, going for a walk and returning to his brother's house to carry out some decoration or repairs once everyone had left for the day. His walk often took him past the café and several times he helped the owner unload a delivery, or as the days got warmer, to put tables and chairs outside.

"Staying for a cuppa?" she said the first time.

When he shook his head, she'd said, "Please do. I make a pot for myself anyway and usually half of it goes to waste." She found excuses to offer him things to eat, too. "This is a new recipe, let me know what you think," and "I made too many of these, don't let them go to waste," or even "eat that bigger one will you? It messes up the display."

Although he guessed she was just being kind and perhaps reading too much into his scruffy appearance and apparently having nowhere to go, Angus couldn't resist the chocolate eclairs, iced buns and fruit scones.

He often stayed to chat. Liz, as he learned she was called, was very easy to talk to. It helped that she didn't know anything about the crash or his life before it. Most of their conversations were about food, but Liz could talk about anything, or nothing. Somehow her words did more to cheer him up than the deliberate attempts of his family to raise his spirits. That's probably why he stayed so long each morning, although receiving a shy smile from the dark haired girl, who had breakfast there a couple of times a week, was an added bonus.

"Are you in a hurry to be off anywhere this morning?" Liz asked one day.

"No, I don't have anything planned," he said. There was

nothing left for him to work on at Donald's house.

"I bought a new picture to go up, but it'll just make the others look grubby. If you'd take them down, give them a wipe and bung them all back up, there'd be eggs and bacon in it for you."

"Make that a cheese omelette and you have a deal."

Angus took the pictures out the back so he could scrub the frames with soapy water to remove a thin film of grease, and give the glass a good polish. When the older pictures were sparkling clean, Angus unwrapped the new one. He revealed a meadow scene full of daisies. They'd had a picnic somewhere like that once. He remembered Daisy hopping about, trying not to step on the flowers which shared her name and then giggling at his attempts to follow in her footsteps without shaking their lunch to pieces. He'd wanted to find her a four leaved clover, but she'd said she didn't need it…

By the time Angus returned, the café was full, every outside chair was occupied and Liz was scribbling in her order pad.

"Their coach got a puncture, so they're having brunch here," Liz explained.

Angus abandoned the pictures and carried jugs of milk, pots of tea and plates of hot food as Liz rapidly grilled, fried, toasted and scrambled almost everything she had in stock.

"I'm sorry your omelette will have to be a small one," she said after the crowd had gone and their tables cleared. "I only have two eggs left." She piled salad onto his plate as well and practically forced scones and the coach party's tips on him.

"You've more than earned it. I'd love to offer you a job but

I can't afford to pay proper wages and don't really need anyone full time."

Angus stared after her back as she went to explain to a newly arrived customer which items were still available.

A job? Of course he could work now. He might never have the confidence to restart his business, but there must be some kind of work he could do. Why hadn't Donald told him to start earning his keep and why hadn't he realised himself that he should be trying to find something?

"How about I work for cakes and you give me a reference when I start applying for jobs?" he suggested.

Angus worked lunchtimes and Saturdays. Occasionally he washed the cafe floor at night and came in first thing to put the tables back in place. Other mornings he'd arrive early to help take in a delivery, wash and refill the flower vases which decorated each table, or do anything else which meant he was still there when the dark haired girl arrived.

It wasn't until Liz asked him to take her order, that he fully realised that was his motivation. Angus wouldn't have spoken to her if he hadn't worked there, but being friendly to customers was part of the job and he wanted to do it well.

After that first time, Angus always took her order and served her, if he was in the café. She seemed shy. Although she never started a conversation, she readily responded to his comments about the weather or things he'd heard on the news and would sometimes add observations of her own.

"I don't really want to know, but how's the job hunting going?" Liz asked on morning, when Angus had stayed later than usual, hoping the girl might appear.

"It isn't. I used to be a decorator with my own small business. That means I don't have references and when I have to explain the business is no longer going, obviously potential employers think I can't have been any good."

"You were though?" Liz guessed.

Angus told her about the accident. Not all of it, not about Daisy. "I'm living with my brother and his family at the moment. They've been brilliant, but there's not really room. I need to find somewhere else, for my sake as well as theirs."

"I can't help myself, but I have an idea."

An influx of customers required attention at that point, so Angus didn't hear her plan until the following day.

"You've met my Aunt Ruth, haven't you?"

"Yes. Lovely lady."

"She is. Quite elderly but still healthy and very independent. She can look after herself perfectly all right, but her house is getting run down. Nothing structural, but there's lots of things which need attention and the whole place could do with a lick of paint. How would you feel about doing some work in exchange for a room of your own?"

"It sounds great if she'd agree to it."

"I asked her yesterday. Aunt Ruth thinks it's a brilliant idea, assuming the two of you get on. She asked for you to go round as soon as you're free and have a chat. To be honest, I think she'd feel happier with someone else about the place."

Angus thought maybe he would too. He had rented a flat for a short while, but Daisy had often stayed over... He'd rather not be reminded how alone he was.

The grass in Ruth's front garden was almost totally covered with daisies. The flowers seemed to be everywhere he went, just as his love had been once. No longer would she use her lunch break to surprise him wherever he was working, rub his shoulders after a hard day or send silly texts to make him laugh during a long, boring project. He almost didn't go in, but Ruth opened the door and called out to him.

Once inside he relaxed. Ruth chattered away very much like Liz always did and it seemed as though she already knew quite a lot about him. He could see there was plenty of work to be done, but probably nothing he couldn't manage.

Ruth showed him around the house. "I was thinking you could have this room here and the box room next to it. As I have my own bathroom, this area would be like a little flat for you. Of course it needs smartening up, but you could decorate to your taste."

"That would be perfect."

They agreed to a month's trial. Angus would work one day a week for his rent and another few hours for which Ruth would pay him the minimum wage. If, after the month, they were both happy they'd make a more formal arrangement.

It worked far better than Angus could have hoped. He enjoyed working on the house and loved having a place of his own without actually being alone. Donald and his family came to visit and once Ruth had met them she regularly invited them to Sunday lunch and encouraged the girls to play in her garden. Angus felt more like a part of his family than he had when he'd been living with them.

One day Ruth said, "Would you mind cutting the grass for me? I can do it, but the mower is heavy and by the time I've finished there's no time to do the things in the garden which I really want to do."

"No problem."

"Don't set it too low though, will you? I don't want you

killing my daises."

He could see a car coming towards him. Too fast! There was nowhere he could go...

Angus felt a hand on his shoulder. "My dear boy, whatever's wrong?"

He realised tears were pouring down his face and, thanks to her concern, the whole story of the crash and his guilt and loss of both Daisy and his confidence poured out of him.

Ruth held his hand until he'd finished talking and his sobs had subsided. "We thought there must be something," she said.

"I'm sorry. Do you want me to leave?" Angus said.

"No. I want you to cut my grass. Come on, I'll show you how the mower works."

She didn't mention his distress again. Liz didn't say anything either, but he had the feeling her aunt had told her.

Angus had almost forgotten the incident until the morning Liz said, "See to the flowers will you?" and handed him not the usual mixed carnations, but a bunch of large pink daisy-like blooms.

"They're just flowers," he told himself. "Not even proper daisies. They don't mean anything." He trimmed the stems and placed three in each of the water-filled vases. He set one on each of the tables and carried the final vase to where the dark haired girl was waiting for her breakfast.

One minute she was smiling as he walked towards her. The next she was drenched in water.

"I'm so sorry," she said as Angus apologised for his clumsiness.

"Come on," Liz said. "I've got a drier out the back for the table clothes. You can borrow an apron whilst it works its magic." She took the girl into the back of the cafe, then returned to Angus.

"It was a warning from Daisy," he said.

"What are you talking about?"

"I liked her. Daisy knows and was keeping me away so I don't hurt her."

"You really believe that?"

Angus had to concentrate to remember what he'd said. "No, no of course not. It was just the shock. Daisies are just flowers and dead people are gone. They can't warn people or well, anything …"

"I'm not so sure about that, but I agree it wasn't a warning. Quite the opposite if you ask me."

"Oh?"

"I think, well Aunt Ruth and I think, she's been trying to heal your hurt. Daisies got you out of hospital. They got you in here and they showed me how useful you are. That gave you a job and then somewhere to live. Now I think they're trying to tell you to be happy."

Angus shook his head. He didn't really believe in ghostly floral messages, good or bad. Especially not bad. Daisy had never been unkind. She'd never have punished him for what wasn't his fault. As his family, and the doctors had said, it was himself who was doing that. It was time he stopped and started living instead.

When the girl returned, Angus brought her a fresh pot of tea and asked if he could take her out. "To apologise for soaking you."

"Yes and no."

She smiled into his puzzled frown.

"Yes I'll come out with you, but it's me who should be apologising. You didn't drop the vase, I somehow managed to knock it out of your hand. Lately I've been seeing daises everywhere. They've sprouted all along the route I walk to get here. When I ordered a dress from a catalogue they sent one with daisy patterns by mistake …"

Angus sat down opposite and tried to make it clear he wanted to hear the whole story.

"The first time was months ago. I found a dropped daisy chain on the ground. Picking it up and wondering how it got there made me miss my usual bus, so I came in here. That was the first time I saw you. Then I noticed daisies everywhere. I started to feel they were a sign and then when I saw you carrying some towards me …" She blushed.

At that moment, the vase, now empty of water, tipped over. They both reached out to save it and instead caught hold of each other's hand.

"It's OK, Daisy," Angus said to himself. "I've got the message at last."

5. Bath Night

"If any of you need the bathroom, get in there quick. I'm going to have half an hour 'me time' and I'm absolutely not to be disturbed."

All three members of Miranda's family immediately decided they needed the facilities. Toby, her son, reminded her he was going out that evening and so, "Could you please not hog the bathroom all evening?"

"The sooner I get in there the sooner I'll be out, so hurry up!"

He was only thirteen, too young to be dating and too young to shave, yet he spent more time in the bathroom than the rest of them combined. If her daughter ever grew out of her tomboy phase, Miranda would need to book her bath night months ahead.

When she finally got in there, she threw the discarded clothing and towels onto the landing. They'd still be out there after her bath she knew, but at least she wouldn't have to tread on them or look at them for the next thirty minutes or so.

Miranda turned on the taps and added moisturising bubble bath to the running water. An extravagant brand, but she deserved it. She'd had such a tough day at the end of a tough week. Two teenage kids to get ready for school, breakfast to make for the whole family and rushing to get the dishwasher stacked so it could run while she was at work. Ditto the washing machine full of school uniform and hubby's work shirts. All day slogging at the computer, food shopping on the way home and then guess who'd be unloading the dishwasher and sorting out the laundry as well as making dinner that evening?

She'd had this little treat planned since Monday morning. Miranda was going to enjoy a nice long soak and a read of her great, great grandmother's diary. Not the original of course. She wouldn't risk that. Fortunately her brother had photocopied it and printed it out for interested family members. Mildred was going to have a bath Miranda had noticed when she'd taken a quick peak at that day's entry over the weekend. That's probably what put the idea in her head.

She'd spent her lunchtimes looking at the website her brother set up, to get an idea of Mildred's life before she started reading. It contained a huge amount of information on their family history, all neatly arranged in chronological order. At the time Mildred had written the entries Miranda planned to read, her great, great grandmother had six children aged from two to fourteen. Six kids! Miranda didn't envy her that. She loved her two and was sure Mildred had loved all hers but two was plenty. No wonder the poor woman wanted a hot bath to relax in.

Miranda did envy Mildred pretty much everything else though. No job for a start. How Miranda would love not to have hers. The money was useful of course and did pay for holidays and other luxuries and she had friends there but it was terribly dull. Then there was Mildred's lovely home and garden. She'd had a thatched cottage with almost an acre of land. Miranda loved her tiny patch of garden and tended it when she could. They sometimes had barbecues or sat out in the evening during summer. But how much better it would be if she could have lots of fruit trees, jut like Mildred did and a vegetable patch and herb garden. She'd often daydreamed of a beautifully chaotic cottage garden full of scented arbours to sit under and a pretty wildflower-filled orchard from which she could pick lush ripe fruit.

As she waited for the bath to fill, Miranda read.

The house always seems so quiet once those who have work or school have left for the day. The place feels so empty when it's just me and the little ones. It's just for a few hours though. How lucky I am that my oldest children have all found places in the factory and haven't had to go into service. I see them every night instead of just on the half day holiday those in big houses get.

Oh gosh, only one of Great Great Gran Mildred's kids were older than Miranda's youngest. She read on.

As usual, my neighbour is watching the little ones whilst I collect our groceries. It was a pleasant walk into town this morning. Once the rain stopped everything looked so fresh and new. It was easy to believe the birds were singing from pure joy.

Miranda sighed. How wonderful to breathe fresh air and hear bird song. Her commute to work was a battle through crowded, polluted streets. The most musical thing she heard was the blaring of angry drivers' horns. Only the calender showed her it was now spring.

She climbed into the warm water, lay back and closed her eyes for a moment. Bliss. Once the tension had eased from her shoulders she continued reading.

Those from the big house travel to London to make many of their purchases, I'm told. I wonder why? Fareham is only two miles away and has such a good choice. Butcher, fishmonger, bakers, grocer; what more could a body possibly want?

Miranda could think of quite a few shops she used that weren't covered by Mildred's list, but things were different then. Women weren't expected to wear makeup, cover grey hairs and dress stylishly for the office. They didn't need coffee to keep them going and a good book to help them relax and of course the mobiles, tablets and the music playing devices Miranda's kids were constantly plugged into just hadn't been invented. She'd love to return to that freedom and simplicity and as for the two mile walk to town, if she had time for that she wouldn't need the gym.

Today the greengrocer had leeks, potatoes in variety, several different cabbages... nothing I can't pick from our own patch or store of course, but it was there for those who hadn't anything left to harvest. That reminds me, this morning I noticed there's a strawberry just showing colour and the pea pods are swelling. Soon we'll be eating those rare delicacies! Talking of rare, Mrs Richard Evans told me that her youngest told her that the family she's with actually ate a pineapple. Imagine! Just hiring one to put on the table to impress his guests cost more than the doctor earned in a week and yet some families were rich enough and soft enough to eat one.

Miranda felt a little guilty at the way she'd complained when her favourite brand of yoghurt hadn't been available in her preferred mango flavour and she'd had to settle for passionfruit. She felt worse still as she read Mildred's account of washing clothes by hand and running them through the mangle before hanging on the line to dry whilst she fed the chickens. To make matters worse, instead of whinging about the task she'd been delighted her husband had helped out by chopping a good pile of logs. Mildred used those on the fire she lit to heat the water she'd fetched from the well!

It almost felt wrong for Miranda to lean forward and allow more hot water to trickle into the bath, but she did it anyway. Poor old Mildred was going to have to carry and heat her water before she'd get to enjoy the soak she clearly deserved more than her great, great granddaughter did.

Just as Miranda was wondering if she'd discover anything she had in common with her ancestor, Mildred declared her love of cake. Miranda had bought cake that very day. She did try to ensure she and the family ate healthily most of the time, but none of them could resist the occasional slice of cake.

Mildred seemed even keener and baked one whenever the hens had laid enough eggs and it seemed that was most days. On the day Miranda was reading about she'd baked what sounded rather like a Victoria sponge though she described it as 'jam cake'. She'd even included the recipe.

Perhaps it is vain of me, but I'm proud of my ability to write. I go so far as to hope my words will outlast me and be of interest to my children and grandchildren.

She must point that bit out to her brother. He'd be so thrilled an ancestor had actually hoped future generations would be interested in family history. Perhaps, if she could find the time, she'd bake that cake for his next visit. The ingredients were all things she could still buy easily enough; eggs, flour, sugar and butter. Miranda was pleased there was no mention in the diary of churning butter and grinding flour. Probably it was the farmers who did that and sold the goods in the grocer's and all Mildred had to do was walk two miles to fetch them. And two miles back.

At last, Miranda read, the children came in from school

and they took the toddler and infant to play while Mildred prepared their supper. She had time, as her husband and older children were still at work. It seemed they had to endure twelve hour days. There was no recipe for the stew and herb dumplings but Mildred still made it sound delicious by mentioning the carrots, swedes and turnips she dug from the garden. She wrote too about the appetising aroma of thyme and parsley leaves plucked fresh from the plants.

The family made short work of the stew and the cake. Then they helped bring in more water and logs so they could wash first the dishes and then themselves. Miranda had been picturing a huge roll top enamel bath, but it soon become clear it was a tin one brought in from an outhouse and set before the fire. Apparently it wasn't emptied and refilled between each user. The kids had the water first starting with the baby. Mildred had gone in after the non working children but before everyone who went to the factory.

Soon we were all clean and dry and sat before the fire. Every day I thank God for my life and my family, but on bath night I feel even more blessed than ever.

Miranda thought of the huge family bible her brother still had. The family's births deaths and marriages were still recorded in it just as they had been in Mildred's day, though that now was their only use for it. That and researching into the past. Miranda remembered reading the names of Mildred's children. There had been another born after the baby who'd got the clean bath water, she remembered. How could she forget? That child had been called Miranda too. She'd chosen to read the particular section of diary she had because Mildred would have been pregnant with her youngest child then. That other Miranda's life was possibly easier than her mothers's but it would still have been hard.

Miranda sank into the lovely deep, hot and scented water. She was never ever going to complain about her own life again. Her thoughts were interrupted by banging.

"Mum, did you hear me?" Toby yelled.

"What is it, Toby?

"The shirt I wanted to wear is all creased, I need you to iron it before you make dinner or I'll be late!"

Miranda sighed then remembered her decision not to complain. Using an electric steam iron was far easier than using the fire-heated, solid smoothing Mildred would have had to contend with. So much easier in fact that a teenage boy could do it.

"Set the ironing board up then," she called. She'd teach him to do his own ironing. That way he'd never need complain she hadn't done it for him and she'd have time to finish reading Mildred's diary.

6. Saying It With Flowers

People kept telling her she'd see Giles again. Anne knew Giles himself had believed that to be true. Was it just wishful thinking which made her think he could be right?

Surely he couldn't have entirely ceased to exist if she loved him as much as ever. Anne could almost hear him in her son's voice, see him in her grandchildren's faces. She talked to him sometimes, especially in his beloved garden. It helped a little. She felt as though he could hear her. A month after she buried him, Anne was certain she'd be with him again one day.

Why wait? She had plenty of painkillers. As she popped the tablets onto a saucer, something outside the window drew her attention. She stepped into the garden and saw the bulbs Giles planted last autumn were peeping through the soil. It was one of the last things they'd done in the garden. She'd been worried he wasn't strong enough, but he said he wanted something for her to look forward to. Giles had known he'd already seen his last spring, but it brought him pleasure to look through the catalogues and place the order.

If she met Giles again soon, he'd like to know the flowers had bloomed.

When she returned to the warmth of the house, Anne saw the packets of painkillers on the side. What had she been thinking? Certainly not of her children. She couldn't end her pain that way and not yet.

Anne hadn't liked to keep calling, to be a burden, but she

rang her daughter to say the bulbs Giles had planted were beginning to show through. It felt good to have a conversation about life and the future, even though it was on such a small scale.

Each day she checked the new shoots and tried to recall what they'd planted. Tulips she remembered but not which varieties. Giles had told her, but the names meant little to her. There were other things too. One she remembered as being something to do with the grandchildren. She recalled the bulbs were different. Tulips were big, shiny and a burnished brown colour, full of promise. The others were smaller, some like hard raisins, some pale and encased in a kind of mesh skin.

The first flowers to bloom were brilliant blue and so beautiful. Anne was glad she'd waited to see them. She could go to Giles now and tell him she'd seen the… Were they iris? Giles had said he'd buy some when their youngest granddaughter was born.

Anne flicked through Giles' old catalogue and discovered she was right, the flowers were a form of iris. There were crosses next to many catalogue entries, looking just like the kisses he used to put on the cards he gave her. Anne touched the cross by the iris and pressed her finger to her lips. She'd wait and see the other bulbs bloom, before she went to Giles.

Next to flower were a rainbow of anemones. They must have been the ones which looked like raisins. Then came the gorgeous tulips. She'd never expected flowers from Giles this birthday, but there were masses of them in her favourite shades of pink and purple. She whispered her thanks to him as though he were right beside her in the garden. Perhaps in a way he was.

The day the last tulip petal fell, Anne felt ready to join

Giles. How; an accident? She walked around the garden and spotted buds on the rose bush. It was the one thing she'd contributed to the garden. It had been on sale, with no label and few leaves, and she'd felt sorry for it. Giles had laughed and said she was as soppy as him.

It hadn't flowered last year. He'd cut it right down to give it the best chance of establishing strong roots and it had sent out plenty of healthy leaves. Now there were lots of buds. Giles would be so pleased if she could tell him it was thriving. He'd ask what colour it was though. What variety. In just a few days she could tell him. She'd wait.

The rose bloomed in a gorgeous range of sunset colours. Palest yellow in the centre, shading through gold and apricot to deep orange at the edge of the petals. The blooms aged to a pinky red colour.

For months friends and family had offered to take Anne out wherever she wanted to go. Always she'd thanked them and declined. She'd just been waiting to go to Giles and she could do that well enough at home. After the rose bloomed she accepted every offer, asking to visit gardens and nurseries to try and identify it.

Anne had no luck. At least not in finding the sunset coloured rose's name. She did spot a hardy geranium to go with it. Sky blue, which seemed appropriate. And wouldn't something providing a froth of white like delicate summer clouds be perfect? The rose had been left without companions until they knew the colour. Once the other plants clothed its bare lower branches and provided contrast for the blooms it looked even better. Every day Anne watered and tended the new plants so they would establish properly and give pleasure for years to come.

One morning she came inside for a cup of tea after doing

that and discovered a new bulb catalogue had arrived. She noticed delicate creamy crocus which would look wonderful with the rich blue iris if, as the catalogue suggested, they flowered at the same time. Anne put a little cross next to tall purple alliums which could rise up through the tulips, and more against several varieties of tulips just because she couldn't resist.

It was a week before she'd convinced herself to place the order. It would take longer than that to plant them all. It would be hard work, but worth it. One day she'd be with her beloved Giles again, but before that she'd see many more flowers grow and blossom. She'd keep them in her memory and take them to share with him.

7. Valentine's Gimmick

Betsie braced herself as she stepped into the office on Valentine's day. She glanced round to check; it hadn't started yet. Good, she'd be able to fortify herself with coffee first. That might help a bit. Looking really busy was her main line of defence though. Betsie kept her gaze on the screen and her hands on the keyboard to discourage anyone from asking her if Tim had brought her breakfast in bed or made any other such silly gesture.

"No," she'd said last year, just keeping from snapping. "I only have a piece of toast in the morning anyway and there's nothing romantic about crumbs in the bed."

That was true. She didn't want Tim to bring her breakfast in bed. Besides he didn't have to resort to gimmicks to show he loved her. She knew. He'd told her several times.

The onslaught began just before ten. A huge bunch of roses arrived for one of the women. The same woman whose husband Betsie had seen in a quiet country pub with a blonde. Betsie thought she ought to give the woman a hint. Probably better not do it today though.

Betsie noticed at the glowing look on the woman's face as she read the cheesy note attached to her bouquet. Maybe she should make enquiries before saying anything. The husband might have to entertain clients as part of his job, or have a sister he socialised with. Betsie shook her head, she wasn't going soft was she?

More gifts arrived during the day. Some were awful

gimmicks. Chocolates costing twice the regular price because they were in a heart shaped box, ghastly, gaudy padded cards and tiny teddy bears which were supposed to be cute but usually weren't. Flowers, even over-priced, imported hot house ones seemed better than that. It seemed silly for them to be sent to the office though. By the time they'd sat crammed together in the bathroom sink all day and the wives or girlfriends struggled home with them, they'd be getting tatty. It was as though everyone had to prove something to the world, not show their love to one special person.

There was one case where Betsie understood the gift not being given in person. One girl only saw her middle-aged boyfriend mid week. She'd never been to his home or met any friends or family. He'd made an excuse not to see her over Christmas too. Betsie was worried he was married and had dropped a few hints to the girl. She'd do it again; but not today.

The lad who delivered the post to all the offices came in just then. She'd given him a hint too. Had he acted on it? Betsie watched. Yes! The pile of mail he added to young Suzy's in-tray contained an oversized envelope in much the same red shade as the lad's face had gone. As he approached Betsie's desk he gave her a sheepish grin and a thumbs up.

"Oh look!" Suzy squealed a few minutes later.

Several of the women clustered round to look.

"Who's it from, Suzy?" They wanted to know.

"I've no idea."

"Of course you have," Betsie said.

"Really I haven't. I don't have a boyfriend."

"Look at the envelope."

"It just says Suzy. That's odd. How did it get here with no stamp?"

"You saw it arrive, didn't you?"

"Yes. But… Oh! Do you think …?"

It was generally agreed the messenger must have been responsible for both delivering and sending it. It wasn't any surprise to anyone when, later in the day, Suzy decided she needed to pop down to the post room.

The real irritations didn't kick in until lunchtime. By then everyone who was likely to receive such a thing had their flowers, cards or chocolates. Three women had been taken out to lunch and another had left to meet her fiancé as they were off to Paris for a couple of days.

"So, did Tim get you anything?" she was asked.

"Yes, he gave me flowers."

"Aaaw, red roses?"

"No. I prefer seasonal flowers."

"Tulips? I love tulips."

"Snowdrops actually. I love snowdrops."

She did. When they'd first started dating it had been autumn. He'd given her chrysanthemums and she'd told him her preference for seasonal flowers. She'd been delighted when he'd given her a pot of living snowdrops on Valentine's Day. She'd planted it in the window box of her bedsit. Each year he gave her more and by the time they started living together three years ago, she'd been able to plant out a nice big patch of them. They were still adding to it.

Conversation then turned to plans for the evening. Most of the women seemed to have arrangements for a meal out. Tim and Betsie didn't go to a restaurant on Valentine's Day. Everywhere was always so crowded that the atmosphere was hardly intimate and romantic.

One woman had plans Betsie approved of.

"We're going to an open evening at the local observatory. My hubby noticed I never miss anything with Brian Cox in, so thought it was a good idea."

"You didn't tell him it was the presenter not the physics you were interested in then?"

She grinned. "It didn't seem tactful. Besides it might be interesting and looking at the stars together is rather romantic, don't you think?"

Betsie and some others agreed.

"And we'll grab a takeaway and bottle of wine on the way home."

That sounded rather nice to Betsie, but it was clear one or two others felt that unless the gesture was expensive, it didn't really count no matter how much thought went into it.

"So, what are you doing, Betsie?"

"We'll have a nice quiet meal in."

"Which you'll have to cook, I suppose."

Betsie was indeed going to cook, but as they were having a ready made pizza it wasn't going to be much of a hardship. After they'd realised the fourteenth of February wasn't the best date for a meal out, they'd decided they'd eat in. They took it in turns to either chose the starter and main course, or desert and wine. That way they both got a surprise and a treat. Often the wine didn't match the meal, as with the full bodied red Betsie had bought the previously year. It wasn't the obvious choice with the king prawn stir fry Tim had made, but neither of them worried about that kind of thing.

"I insist on being taken somewhere luxurious for any special occasions and being given a nice piece of jewellery,"

Betsie was told. "You really should get that man of yours trained."

She felt like replying, "And you should treat yours better so he doesn't sneak out to meet blondes," but instead she asked, "And what do you do for him?"

"Me? Do? I don't follow."

"Isn't it Valentine's day for him too?"

Betsie and Tim's relationship was a true partnership. Special occasions were a reason to celebrate together, not for one to spend money on the other. Any spare cash they had went towards paying a bit more off the mortgage, not on a silly bit of jewellery. Not that all jewellery was silly; there was one piece Betsie would very much like to have. Still, she didn't need it. She knew Tim loved her and hadn't they proved their commitment to each other by buying the house?

As Betsie left work that evening, she saw something that she felt symbolised the true meaning of Valentine's Day. The post boy was stood outside looking a little vulnerable. Betsie smiled at him and his face seemed to explode into a grin. Not at her, she didn't think he'd even noticed her. He was smiling at Suzy skipping down the steps to meet him. They exchanged a few words and turned to walk away together. As Betsie watched them go, Suzy reached out to take hold of the boy's hand. She mentally wished them well, then went home to her beloved Tim.

Before she unlocked the front door she bent down to sniff the pot of snowdrops in the porch. They had a sweet, subtle fragrance. Perfect. She had a quick shower, put on her slinkiest dress and went down to lay the table.

Tim came home, kissed her, then put a bag in the fridge. "Don't look yet," he said then went to get changed himself.

She had the starter prepared, fresh basil picked, and oven on by the time her returned.

"Something smells good, what are we having?"

"Inspired by the prawns you cooked last year, we're having some for a starter. Just a few sizzled in garlic butter. Then the pizza."

"Looks good. Is that black olives and mascarpone I can see?"

"Of course!"

"You know me so well, love."

"Let's see if you know me as well... Something chocolatey for dessert? Or with fruit, or cream." She laughed. "Actually as long as you got some kind of dessert you can't have gone wrong, can you?"

"That's what I thought. We've got chocolate cheesecake... and strawberries and cream."

"Mmm, double points!" She kissed him. "We'd better get started if we're going to get through all that."

"Why don't we have a drink first?"

"Yes, OK. Is everything all right, love?"

"Yes." He didn't sound positive. "I really should have got red to go with the pizza."

"White will go with the prawns though," she pointed out.

"True. I'll get the glasses."

Betsie opened the fridge to look for the wine. It wasn't ordinary white wine, but sparkling. Lovely. Oh, champagne! That'd be something to tell them at work. She hoped he hadn't spent too much. Any champagne was expensive and as this was done up with a fancy silver ribbon it was surely no exception.

What was that on the ribbon? She was studying it as Tim placed the glasses on the table. It looked just like a diamond ring. Another silly gimmick. Probably Tim hadn't seen that, or he'd not have bought it. What an irresponsible thing to decorate a bottle with, especially on Valentine's Day. Some women given that would get entirely the wrong idea.

Betsie was just wondering whether to say anything to Tim, or just remove the ribbon and keep quiet when she noticed he was crouched down. He'd seemed quiet since he'd come home. What a shame if he had indigestion. They could keep the food until tomorrow, but it wouldn't be quite the same.

Tim reached for her hand. She'd started to help him up when the truth dawned on her. He wasn't crouched in pain, but on one knee looking nervous.

"Betsie, will you marry me?"

"Yes. Oh definitely, yes!"

He stood up and pulled her into his arms. Some time later he slipped the ring on her finger. It was too big.

"I thought it might be," Tim said. "I wanted you to be able to put it on for tonight though. The shop gave me a thing to check your size and they'll either make this fit or swap it for one which does."

"I want it to be this one."

"Good. Me too. I'll take it in tomorrow, it will take a few weeks to have it altered though."

"No problem." She'd have nothing to show them at work in the morning. Nothing that is except the huge grin on her face, bounce in her step and sparkle in her eyes. Those who didn't think that was what was most important weren't worth impressing anyway.

8. On A Summer Day

She lay on her back in the fragrant meadow, her face pillowed on uncut hay. Her troubles were as small and far away as the tiny clouds she guessed were drifting lazily high above them. The sun felt as warm and soft as her husband's gentle caress.

Another bite from the peach caused rich, sweet juice to run down her neck. Pretending annoyance, she wiped it away. "If you see a wasp I don't want to know."

"I see only you." He tasted the ripe fruit on her lips.

A flurry of activity reminded her they weren't alone. The children brought her a posie of wildflowers. She bent her head to the poppies, cornflowers and moon daisies. Her blind eyes couldn't see the bright colours, but she could hear them in her children's laughter and the skylark's song.

9. Roundabout Rose

Nigel looked around the garden centre. This was a bad idea. Buying rose bushes was far more complicated than blooms from the florist. He must chose between bush, standard and shrub forms, climbing roses, Floribunda, Hybrid Tea...

A voice cut through his doubts. "Nigel? How lovely to see you!"

"Linda. What a surprise." When he'd retired, they'd hugged and promised to keep in touch. He hadn't meant it. Not because he hadn't enjoyed his secretary's cheerful company and mildly flirtatious banter or appreciated her neat figure and warm smile, but because he had.

He'd even teased his wife, Rose, that she had competition.

"Don't believe you! You only love me."

"You've got your thorns stuck in so far I can't escape you mean," he'd retorted. She'd known he was joking, hadn't she? He was fairly sure she had, and that Rose liked Linda.

"Thank Linda for me," Rose, realising who'd advised him, said whenever Nigel got it right over a birthday or Christmas present.

"So, have you taken up gardening?" Linda asked now. "Or are you buying a present for that lucky wife of yours?"

"Neither really... I'm planting a rose bush in her memory."

"Oh, Nigel. I'm so sorry. I had no idea."

"It was quick."

In those last few days, Rose was so brave.

"I don't want you moping around, you know... afterwards," she'd said. "See friends. Have fun, like we always have. And I don't want a grave and a headstone. Scatter my ashes somewhere we went together. Preferably somewhere you're not supposed to do that kind of thing."

He'd had her cremated, but not been able to follow her other wishes. Almost a year later, on what would have been her birthday, Nigel had bought flowers and put them next to her urn. He'd felt Rose's disapproval.

He'd decided to buy a rose bush, plant it on the roundabout at the end of the road and sprinkle her ashes there. He and Rose had driven around it whenever they went anywhere and he was sure the general public weren't supposed to dig holes in roundabouts.

He didn't tell Linda the details of his plan, just, "I want something tough, yet beautiful."

Linda helped him chose the perfect plant, with cheerfully bright flowers. As Nigel headed for the till he wished he'd suggested getting a cup of tea. It would have been nice to chat with Linda, but he'd lost the chance.

"Ouch!" The tough, beautiful shrub had dug a thorn into him.

Linda, hearing his cry of pain, returned to check he was OK.

"I'm fine. Just a scratch."

It was, but also a reminder his Rose wasn't far away. How could he have thought to betray her like that?

Nigel paid for the rose, carried it to his car and put it on the front seat. He somehow dislodged the label which blew away. By the time Nigel caught up with it, he was in the entrance to the garden centre's cafe. Feeling Rose was trying to tell him something, he found a seat and studied the label.

Nigel learned that to give his bush the best start, he needed something called mycorrhizal fungus.

"Hello again. Mind if I join you?" It was Linda.

"Please do." Rose would have wanted him to be polite at least, he was sure of that.

After they'd ordered tea and scones with cream and jam, Nigel showed Linda the label. "Is this fungus stuff any good?"

"Sometimes plants need something to help start them off, a bit of encouragement if you like."

Could Rose be doing that to him, with the thorn and flyaway label?

"Would you like me to help plant it?" Linda offered.

"You might not want to." Nigel told her where he would place it and that he didn't intend to obtain permission.

"Guerilla gardening? What fun!"

As the waitress placed the pretty, rose-patterned tea things on the table, Nigel remembered exactly what his wife had said; that he shouldn't mope, but have fun and meet up with friends.

"Yes, I think it will be," he said. "We'll have to do it after dark though, so shall we have dinner somewhere first. Build up our strength and nerve?"

"I'd like that."

Nigel knew Rose would be shaking her head, but only because it had taken him so long to get the message.

10. Holiday Temptations

Holidays are great. I don't mean mine, I never take one, but I do so enjoy those taken by you and your friends. Everyone relaxes; no matter how prim or sensible they usually are, everyone lets down their guard a bit when they escape to the sun for a week or two. Skirts will be shorter, tops cut lower. Sensible shoes and socks swapped for light airy sandals. You stay out later, take a little less care, ignore a few of the rules. That's all right, this is a nice safe resort, there's little to harm you here.

It's good for you to get a break from work, responsibilities and cold, miserable, wintry weather. Alcohol helps too of course and so does the party atmosphere. You'll be dancing until dawn with recently acquired best friends, bodies close in crowded discos and nightclubs. It doesn't matter what language you speak. Laughter, a raised glass, suggestive wink, these things require no translation. Speech is useless anyway over speakers used to maximum effect. It's too loud to hear the music, you feel instead the rhythm pulsing through your body. Those cheerful songs drown out other, more irritating sounds.

I am watching you, aware of your movements, aware of the heat rising in every limb and the sweat glistening on your tender skin. I move around the packed room, there are so many fit young bodies here it's difficult to know where to start, but I like the look of you. Your pale flesh makes you look so sweet and vulnerable. Don't worry that you are an easy target, you'll mean no less to me because of that. There will be many others over the summer season but you will be my first. Perhaps I will be yours?

Let us breathe in the intoxicating mix of perfume and cocktails, cigarette smoke mingling with, but not masking, the exotic flowers from the club's lush tropical garden. Gardenia, star jasmine and lemon blossom waft in, whenever there's the slightest breeze.

You must be thirsty, I know I am. Why don't you taste the drinks? There's cold refreshing lager, its bubbles bursting on your tongue. Perhaps you will try something new, a brightly coloured liqueur in a tall glass, glinting enticingly over crushed ice. Perhaps you would prefer a sophisticated Gin and tonic with a slice of lime. You decide, it's all the same to me.

At the first light of dawn the music ends, the bar staff stop serving and the doors open. The sudden quiet disorientates us for a moment before the mass of bodies drift apart back to their hotels. Maybe they'll be sleeping alone, maybe not. Bodies sprawled out, or closely entwined, naked, perhaps with a cotton sheet dragged over. They dream alone, or make love together, or just wait for breakfast.

I will be with you now as you relax on the comfortable bed. I'll admire the beginnings of a tan on your soft skin. Those hours spent at the gym in preparation for your fortnight in the sun haven't gone unnoticed. You are rightly proud of your body. I'm not the only one to appreciate your gentle curves.

Windows are thrown open wide to allow in early morning's cool refreshing breeze and the lingering, heavy scent of night blooming flowers. I'll go now, but I'll not forget you. There will be other nights together before you

In The Garden Air

leave.

There you are, spit roasting on the beach, basting regularly with oils, turning for an even result if sleep has not claimed you. All that exposed flesh offering me a constant temptation. You are over heated and sweating from the unaccustomed humidity, but I don't mind. The sun is what you came here for, you should enjoy it.

Shade is a luxury here, if you want relief from the heat you must look for it. You might go wandering through the tropical gardens, where the huge paddles of banana, airy fronds of tree ferns and brilliantly striped cannas work their magic. Perhaps you'll opt to be refreshed by sparkling fountains. No...

I think you'd prefer to sit for a while, relaxed and at peace by still water. Imagine the brilliant blue flowers and floating pads of giant waterlilies and rafts of pretty water hyacinth. The cool, still depths, mirroring your beauty and that of the leaves and blossom around you. I'll be there waiting, we know where to find each other don't we?

There will be busy days shopping in noisy dirty towns. You can search for a souvenir to take home, and a gift for your mum. You must go sight seeing, this land is rich in culture, and there is much to see. With luck you'll photograph an iridescent hummingbird sipping nectar from an open bloom. Long journeys are enjoyed or endured on over crowded coaches. My kind and yours will meet constantly, join together briefly before going on to someone new. Holidays are like that. We know the rules, make the most of each and every opportunity. There's no time to form long relationships. No time for regrets.

Back now at the hotel there's just time for a drink before getting changed for dinner. Go for a stroll in the hotel gardens; sit for a moment by the tranquil pool. You will find me there. You will always find me waiting there.

The holiday is over and you go, I stay. You will not forget me at least, not for a while. Your sweet tender flesh will still feel my touch. Did you keep track to make comparisons with your friends at the airport? It doesn't matter if you didn't. You could just count the itchy red swellings to see how often we were together. I hope to meet you again, perhaps I will, or maybe next year you will remember the insect repellent.

11. A Little Less Self Restraint

Grace watched the starlings splashing around in the birdbath. She knew they only did it because they needed to keep their plumage in good condition or risk perishing on frosty nights, but it looked as if they were having fun. If she'd dared think of Simon, she'd have imagined him laughing at the sight.

Once the starlings flew away, she went out to replenish the water.

"They've never drunk it all?" her neighbour Ruth called.

Grace explained why the water had so quickly been used up.

"Oh! I hadn't thought of them actually bathing. That explains it. Grace, are you sure we can't persuade you to see the New Year in with us tonight?" Ruth asked.

Grace managed a small smile. She couldn't see what was so special about New Year's Eve. She stayed up to see in the New Year because it was traditional, not because she felt the need for late night drinking and partying.

"Thank you, no. I have been invited to my niece's home." That much was true, even if Grace had no intention of accepting.

Ruth looked relieved. "Oh, how nice. Well, have a lovely time and good luck with your resolutions!"

Resolutions were another thing Grace didn't bother with. So many people thought they could change themselves overnight. They promised to give up smoking or go on a diet. Grace didn't need to; she'd never smoked and was the right weight. All people needed was a little self restraint. That should be their resolution and not just for a few days. She was used to seeing joggers in the park opposite at the start of January, but they all gave up long before Valentine's.

After lunch, Grace took the crusts from her sandwich out for the birds. If she was lucky, the starlings would be back again that afternoon. It was always a joy to watch them whether they were hunting for grubs in the lawn, squabbling over scraps on the table, or splashing about in the water.

Ruth was still in her garden, hanging out children's clothes, when Grace went out again.

"Have you seen a robin yet?" Ruth called.

"No, I haven't."

On Christmas Eve, Grace had agreed with Ruth that it would be nice to see a robin. She was almost regretting that now as Ruth had somehow managed to persuade her it was possible and in the days since, Grace had been hopeful of getting a new visitor to the food supplies she put out.

It was as silly to make a fuss about one bird, when she saw so many others, as it was to make more of a fuss over one evening in the year. She was fine at home on her own, just as she always was, Grace thought, as she sipped a small sherry that evening. She drank slowly, so it would last long enough for her to make a quiet toast at midnight.

Big Ben struck twelve. Grace lifted her glass, whispered, "I remember you, Simon my love," and finished the sherry. She watched the celebrations on TV; all those people in Trafalgar Square kissing strangers, then grabbing hands to sing Auld Lang Sine. It was a silly overreaction, but it did look like fun.

There were fireworks in the park outside Grace's home. She watched from her window and listened to the laughter. It looked very pretty and people were clearly enjoying themselves. Just for a moment she regretted ignoring the flyer, stuffed through every letterbox on the estate, inviting residents to join in. Then Grace remembered that watching television was sufficient excitement just before going to bed.

Grace's doorbell rang.

"We saw your light on," Ruth said. "Everything OK?"

"Er, yes. I didn't go to my niece in the end ..." She trailed off, unsure how to explain without either lying or hurting Ruth's feelings, neither of which she wished to do. Young Emily had been almost angry that afternoon when Grace refused yet another invitation. She'd said she wished she hadn't bothered asking. It was only then that Grace realised sticking to her simple routine affected anyone other than herself.

"That's a shame," Ruth said. "Still it means you can come round to us for a drink to see in the New Year now. Come on, if we're quick we can make a toast before this year is an hour old."

Grace intended to refuse and go straight to bed, but somehow she was next door, drinking sparkling wine and saying 'Happy New Year' to Ruth's family, neighbours and friends.

"So, any resolutions, Grace?" Ruth asked.

She meant to say 'no' because she didn't need any. Because her life was fine just as it was. Instead, she found herself saying, "I'm going to give up denying myself every little treat, just because I no longer have Simon to share them with."

"Simon?" Ruth gently asked.

"My husband." She could have explained how much she missed him, how much fun he'd been, how he loved this time of year and the promise of a fresh start each January. Instead she raised her glass and said, "I'm enjoying sharing this little party with you all."

"Great, then you'll come round to tea next week?"

The children would probably make too much noise and Grace would be pressed into eating a little more than she strictly needed, but she couldn't refuse. She'd made a resolution and so she should stick to it. Routine and tradition were important, otherwise who knew where she'd end up?

"Thank you, I'd like that very much," she said. "I've just thought of another resolution; I'm going to buy some mealworms and see if I can entice a robin in time for next Christmas."

"Oh, lovely idea!"

Tomorrow Grace would ring Emily, apologise for not coming for New Year and ask if she could please accept the standing invitation to Sunday lunch for the first time since she was widowed. She might be served a strange foreign dish instead of a proper roast, but it wouldn't hurt her to try something different just the once. For now though, she finished her glass of wine, a mince pie and three chocolate coins before going home to bed.

12. The Perfect Line

I'd never had much confidence talking to girls. I'd get nervous and blurt out, "Love your new hair," to someone on their way to the salon, say their or even my own name wrong, or dry up and try express myself using only my eyebrows.

Talking to the women at work was fine. Until recently they were all married or twice my age.

"Maybe that's why, Paul?" my sister suggested. "Because you're not interested in a relationship you aren't worried about messing up your chances?"

"You're probably right."

My sister is OK, I can talk to her but I've always known her and obviously I'm not romantically interested in her. Alice understands my shyness. That's not always helpful.

I recently asked what she thought was the most appealing thing I could say to a girl.

"I must be going?"

"There must be some way I can make my chat up lines better."

"There is," Alice said.

"Go on."

"Get someone else to say them."

She eventually relented and said, "It's not so much what the man says, but how he says it and who he is."

"I'm me which isn't good and my delivery is bad, so what I say is all I have going for me."

"You're not so terrible really," she said quite kindly. "And you might get better with practise."

"Who can I practise on?"

"How about my mates? They like a laugh."

I could talk to Alice's friends – sort of. Usually it was, "Hello," when I opened the door followed by, "She's up in her room." I didn't pursue the idea.

Then Trina started work. I really liked her. Anyone would. She's quite pretty but that's not why. Trina's just really, really nice. I could talk to her. OK I said stupid things sometimes, like the time I made coffee and asked, "Would you like some Trina, sugar?" but she didn't roll her eyes like I was an idiot.

Actually, just to show there were no hard feelings the next time she made coffee she said the same to me. "Would you like some Trina, sugar?"

I decided then and there to ask her out. Chances were she'd say no, but she'd do it politely and there was the slimmest chance she'd agree. We had a few things in common; we liked the same kind of music, were both vegetarians and enjoyed walking. I could suggest a walk followed by a vegetarian lunch somewhere. She'd mentioned a pub someone had told her served good food and which was near a nature reserve. That would be perfect.

Obviously I didn't actually ask her then and there. I still didn't know how.

I asked Alice to arrange a practise session. She's nothing like me so got on the phone straight away and asked four friends to help.

"What do I say?" I asked.

Alice said. "Try anything you can think of and see how it goes."

I knew plenty of lines, as I'd done an internet search. They were all terrible.

"Did it hurt when you fell from heaven?" I asked friend A.

She rolled her eyes.

"Do you know what people say behind your back?" I tried on B.

"What?"

"Nice ass."

She giggled.

"Would you like to borrow my phone?" I asked C.

"I've got my own," C said.

That wasn't the response I'd expected, but I adapted my reply. "Then call home and say you'll be late back."

Another eye roll was my reward. It wasn't surprising. They were so obviously pick up lines that they'd only work if I'd been super confident, which I think I've established isn't the case.

Friend D got my last attempt. "Here's £20. Drink until I'm good looking, then give me a wave."

That got another giggle.

Funny was best, but still awful. I was sure no line would work unless the girl was already interested and then it wouldn't really matter what I said. Alice and her friends agreed.

On Saturday Alice offered more advice. "A girl doesn't want to hear a line you'd say to anyone. She wants you to be interested in her, say something just to her."

"I can't. Spontaneity isn't really my thing." Actually that's not quite true. I often blurt stuff out spontaneously, just not the sort of thing that's likely to impress a girl.

There was a knock at the door.

"Get that will you?" Alice said.

I opened to door to a huge box of vegetables, held almost at head height.

"Wow, nice butternut squash," I said spotting my favourite cooking ingredient.

"Thanks." The box descended and I saw Trina.

"Er, um ..."

"Take the box and ask her in," Alice prompted.

I did.

Alice introduced us as though we'd never met, then said, "Trina told me she'd grown too many vegetables and I said my veggie brother would be glad of some."

"Thanks, Trina. It all looks delicious."

That explained the squash, but not how they'd come to have the conversation. Fortunately I seemed to have said the right thing as Trina grinned.

Alice offered her a coffee. As she made it she said, "Paul and I were just talking about a girl he fancies at work and he's been practising the perfect way to ask her out."

"Oh really?" Trina asked.

I wanted to hide. She had to know it was her Alice was talking about.

"They're all dreadful," Alice said. "Go on, try some on Trina."

Awkward. Obviously I wanted to chat her up, but I didn't want to use awful lines on her, then again I didn't want to refuse to try chatting her up. "Um... Get your coat, you've pulled."

They both groaned.

"Do you believe in love at first sight, or shall I walk by again?"

Trina giggled.

"I'd like to rearrange the alphabet and put U and I together."

"They really are dreadful." Trina was laughing with, rather than at, me I thought.

"At least I didn't say, nice dress, can I talk you out of it? Er, except now I have."

"As I'm wearing trousers, I'll forgive you. Do you have more of these?"

"Lots." My internet research had been very thorough. "Your father must have been an alien, because you're more lovely than anything on Earth." Then, because once I'd got started I didn't know how to stop, I tried, "I need the kiss of life because you've taken my breath away."

Trina's got a delightful laugh. She is delightful.

"My magic watch says you're not wearing underwear. Oh, my mistake, it's an hour fast."

She pretended to slap my face, but her touch was more like a caress. I was right about her. She really was nice.

"Be unique and different; say yes."

After a few more she said, "OK, Paul I give in. You can stop now."

It was about then I realised Alice had vanished and I'd been talking to Trina with no back up and it had been fine. More than fine. Flirting could almost have described how I was behaving. How we were behaving.

"You were warned they were terrible."

"That's true," she agreed.

"A line like that wouldn't be the best way to ask you out, would it?"

"Not really, but I've heard worse."

"Really?"

"Maybe not worse exactly, but less appealing."

That was vaguely encouraging. "So what would be better? Alice said it should be something spontaneous and said just to that one girl."

"She's right."

"That's OK in theory, but I still don't know what to say."

Trina gave me a thoughtful look. "You could compliment her butternut squash."

"That's not a chat up line!"

"That depends on who says it. Go on, be brave."

"You've got lovely butternut squash, Trina. Will you come out with me please?"

"Thank you. I'd love too."

"Really?"

"Yes, really. How about tomorrow?"

I could only nod.

"We can go for a walk round the nature reserve and then have lunch in that restaurant I was telling you about."

"Excellent. Yes. Good."

She kissed my cheek and left.

I stayed where I was for a while wondering if it had all been a weird dream. Then I picked up one of the butternut squash. It was heavy, definitely real. That meant I really had asked Trina out and she'd said yes. I went in search of Alice.

"Hey, Sis! You'll never guess what. Trina's the girl from work I was telling you about."

"No kidding!"

"You knew?"

She gave me that look which is universal code for 'my little brother is a complete idiot'. Alice must have tracked her down, befriended her and persuaded her to come round.

I hugged her.

"What was that for?"

I explained what I thought she'd done.

"I absolutely did not. What kind of weirdo stalks girls for her brother?"

That was a good point.

"So how did you meet?"

"She spotted us in the supermarket together last week. Remember you took everything home and I met up with my friends?"

"Yes."

"She came over and asked if I was your sister or girlfriend. The six of us hatched a plan."

"Your friends all knew?"

"Told you they like a laugh. Aww, don't look like that. After what we put you through, talking to Trina tomorrow shouldn't be too difficult."

You know, I think she's right.

13. Faraway Friends

Dear Jean, thanks for your last email. I'm so pleased you've settled in so well and that life in Canada suits you. Sounds like you're having a ball. Certainly looks like it from the photos and aren't your grandchildren cute?

I'm missing you of course, but I took your advice about joining in a few things and I've made a new friend. The new vicar's wife! She's a bit shy (makes a change for me to be the brave one!) We like the same books, that's how we got friendly – we joined a reading group. We both read more than the others so have started meeting for coffee and chatting about those which aren't on the group's list. Julie, that's the vicar's wife's name, had a daughter late in life too and like mine she lives away. Not as far away as you and yours though!

Talking of Elissa, she's coming down this weekend and bringing Claude. I'm sure I've told you about him because she met him before you moved (still can't think of it as emigrating – sounds so far and so final!) He's a doctor, Claude I mean. I'm really looking forward to meeting him. I think he might be The One! Maybe in a couple of years I'll have grandchildren photos to send to you?

Your friend on the other side of the world, Suzie.

Dear Jean, Thanks for all the messages and pictures. Sorry it's taken me so long to reply. I'm fine, but I've had things on my mind.

I'll be in touch soon. Do send more pictures, it does me good to see you so happy.

Yours, Suzie.

Dear Jean, Please don't worry about me. I'm OK really. Just a little low perhaps. No, I've not seen much more of Julie. She's nice enough, but what do I have in common with a vicar's wife?

Elissa came as planned and she's very well. Sends her best. And yes, I've met Claude now. He's lovely except the Australian accent. Well, it's not the accent I mind so much, it's just that obviously he's an Australian which means his home is in Australia. Elissa never said. The worst of it is he's so nice that she might marry him. Australia's so far! It doesn't seem fair. First losing my husband, then my oldest and best friend moving away, and now perhaps my daughter too.

I hope she knows what she's doing. Nice as he seems he's not perfect. I don't want her to uproot and find out he's no good.

I wish you were still just down the road.

Your faraway friend, Suzie.

Dear Jean, I'm sorry about my last emails. I was feeling sorry for myself. Well, you'd worked that out, hadn't you? In truth there's nothing wrong with Claude. Elissa's brought him to see me a couple of times and he's been quite charming, even though I admit I've done my best to sabotage their relationship. Tell the truth that's probably why I didn't contact you for a while – I'm feeling a little ashamed. I'll give you an example. He always brings me lovely flowers and instead of thanking him I tell Elissa he wastes money.

That's just the tip of the iceberg. I keep having little digs about him and hate myself for it. Worse is that I'm making Elissa unhappy. She doesn't talk to me so much now and doesn't stay long, especially when Claude is with her.

My behaviour has kept me away from Julie too. I haven't told her all of it, but I did say I'd behaved badly. She was great. Kidded me a bit, saying I could do penance for my sins by helping her with the church flowers. Remember all the shrubs in my garden were getting overgrown? We hacked them right back and Julie took some bits away for her arrangements. I think I've attached before and after pictures.

Your reports and photos of the Rockies were brilliant by the way. That bit about the bear made me laugh so much and I really needed that. I miss you. I feel bad that I've not asked about you and your family much – please send all your news.

Your unworthy friend, Suzie

Dear Jean, what fantastic pictures! You really put my efforts to shame. Your grandchildren are absolutely adorable and don't they grow! Amazing to think they're using tricycles already. Seems only days ago our daughters were out on theirs, doesn't it? Remember that year we each bought our girl an identical pink bicycle and then, so we could tell one from another, we both went and bought the same accessory set? We were in fits but they just rolled their eyes at us.

Thank you so much for your last message. You were right of course, I'm not such a bad person, even though I've behaved badly. I couldn't explain to Elissa, but I did apologise. The only way I could think of saying I didn't really dislike Claude was to say her Dad would have liked him. He would too. Elissa hugged me and said there was nothing to forgive.

Claude wasn't with her but I asked her to bring him next time. I'll cook him a nice meal.

I took your advice too about Julie, the vicar's wife, and have spent more time with her. She gave me a lovely ginger cake recipe which I've copied out below. I warn you though, it's a bit too lovely! We've decided we'd better join a keep fit class or something.

Your bigger than when you saw her last friend, Suzie

Dear Jean, Well thanks very much! Not a word about missing me I notice, just a lot of drooling over cake!

I've attached a few pictures of the cakes and biscuits we've been eating. The first one is a really gooey chocolate cake with a secret ingredient – beetroot! Sounds mad but tastes wonderful. Then there's the ginger cake, scones, Easter biscuits with lemon icing and my Sunday roast. There are some of Elissa and Claude too.

Ha ha! Suzie

p.s. No, Julie hasn't got me sewing kneelers for the church! Cheeky moo. It's over 50 years since I sewed that button through my work and onto my uniform skirt in homecraft lessons and you're still going on about it from the other side of the world. No, it's just the book chat we share and a bit of flower arranging – well that and a lot of home made cakes during the discussions. We take it in turns to bake.

p.p.s Hope you're enjoying your elk burgers or whatever it is you eat over there.

Dear Jean. Thanks for the elk burger recipe. Next time elk steaks are on special offer down the high street I'll be sure to try it.

Flower arrangement pictures attached. Bet you can tell which are mine and which are Julie's. You remember me mentioning Julie? She's my NICE friend! The one who doesn't remind me of every single embarrassing thing I've ever done!

Yours mightily miffed, Suzie

Dear Jean, oh dear just realised I accidentally attached dozens of pictures of cakes to my last message. Oooops!

Ha ha. Suzie.

Dear Jean, Elissa's coming this weekend and she says she has something to tell me. Either she's split with Claude or she's going to marry him. Wish me luck either way? I can't even hope for one outcome as my daughter broken hearted is no improvement on her blissfully happy on the other side of the world.

Your worried friend, Suzie

Dear Jean. He proposed, she turned him down and it's all my fault! She says she knows I'm not fond of Claude and that I'm such a good judge of character that must mean there's something wrong with him. I've put her right, at least I hope I have. I was wrong that her miserable at home would be as bad as her happy in Australia. It's far, far worse.

Your unhappy friend, Suzie

Dear Jean. They're engaged! I'm happy for them, really I am. She was glowing and I remembered how I felt when I married her dad. I'm so relieved not to have messed everything up! He'll make a great husband I'm sure and haven't the two of us proved it's easy for people to stay in touch these days, wherever they happen to live?

They want to get married in the local church – Julie's nearly as thrilled about that as I am and is already planning the flowers.

You'll get a proper invitation of course but to give you an idea they're thinking October time. I do hope you can come – and stay for a while too. There'll be no problem putting you up. And I've been thinking about your suggestion that I visit you… make a good stop over on a trip to Australia, don't you think?

Your, just a plane ride away friend, Suzie

14. Shopping Lists

I pulled out three trolleys to get the one with a piece of paper wedged in the child seat. As I'd guessed, it was a shopping list.

I love other people's lists and pick up any I see. An odd hobby, I know, but harmless. The first time I did it was when I'd left my own at home. A woman returned her trolley as I went to take one.

"Thanks," I murmured as I placed my hands where hers had been.

I'd got Janet settled in the seat before I saw the list abandoned in the bottom of the trolley. The woman had looked about my age and had a child with her, so our needs were likely to be similar. Her list could substitute for mine, I reasoned. I was right; together with my memory it helped me buy what I needed.

It was some time before I looked at anyone else's shopping list. I picked one up to put in the nearby litter bin. The list was very short but the receipt, folded around it, had an alarmingly high total. As I shopped, I entertained myself by daydreaming about being able to afford the fancy wines and cheeses the other shopper had bought.

Lists, whether of intended or actual purchases, reveal a lot about a person. I didn't write them as a child, but if I had they'd have been for sweets for the first few years, then anything to do with the pony I'd desperately wanted. Later I spent my money on magazines, clothes and makeup. The first real lists I made were for my wedding. After that came ones concerned with the needs of a baby. The lists grew longer as our family grew, then shortened again as the children moved away.

I occasionally saw the woman whose list I'd used back when Janet was a baby. I'm fairly sure it was the same person. The contents of her trolley provided a rough reflection of mine. When I shopped for a family it seemed she did too. As I bought less, so did she.

Occasionally we exchanged a few words. Usually just, "Sorry," when one of us was blocking a section of shelving the other wished to reach, but sometimes we had an actual conversation.

"They've reduced a lot of things in the bakery section, did you see?" I said.

"Thanks. I might find something to fill lunch boxes without emptying my purse," she replied.

Her lists, I imagined, would still look much like my own.

I've left out an important one though. Not a paper list, but one that's stuck in my memory. My daughter Janet was seeing a boy I wasn't quite sure about. He was polite, nice looking, charming. He had a good job as a chef which provided him with a flat over the restaurant. He seemed too good to be true. When, the day Janet was due to go to dinner at his place, I saw him in the supermarket, that was too good an opportunity to miss. He wasn't following a list. He didn't drop his receipt. He did however accept my offer of a lift home and I accepted his offer of coffee.

That gave nosy me the chance to see what he'd bought. His bag held the ingredients for the meal, proving he didn't steal from his employer. He'd bought Janet's favourite flowers and chocolates, proving he was romantic and paid attention to her preferences. A single bottle of, not very strong, sparkling wine showed he wasn't intending to get her drunk. At the bottom was a pack of condoms which I pretended not to notice. They've been married twelve years now and are very happy.

When I retired I didn't use the supermarket. My husband and I bought food from farm shops, street markets and unusual delicatessens. We didn't bother with lists as we never knew what we might find.

The worst lists I've ever made weren't for items I wished to acquire, but for those I had to dispose of after my husband died. It was a terrible time, but my children and their spouses were a tremendous help.

It was some time before I went shopping on my own again. I went without a list as I didn't need very much and only had myself to please. If I forgot anything it wouldn't matter; returning the following day would give me the chance to talk to someone, even if it was only to say I could manage my own packing.

That's when my interest in shopping lists and receipts really took hold. I picked up every one I saw and tried to guess about the list maker and what they had planned for the week ahead. Silly perhaps, but it amused me.

I'd decided to challenge myself to buy things on my latest found list and make a meal from them when I saw the woman I'd come to think of as my list twin. She dropped a pack of painkillers into her basket. It landed on a stack of similar packs, next to a bottle of wine.

"Hello," I murmured, wondering if it was too late to form a friendship.

She turned away without speaking and headed for the checkout. There was no need to see the receipt to know she'd bought nothing but wine and tablets. There had been times, just after I was widowed, when I'd considered making the same purchases and consuming the items all together. I followed, not sure what to do or say, but knowing I couldn't let her walk away alone.

"Please wait," I said as she paid.

She looked at me in surprise. I don't think she'd realised I was there. She did wait though.

"Do you have time for a coffee or something?" I asked.

She checked her watch. "I've got twenty minutes."

That reassured me a little about the contents of her shopping bag. If they'd been for what I imagined she'd either have felt she had no time to waste, or been in no hurry at all.

By the time we were sipping drinks in the supermarket cafe, it felt like Sue and I were old friends.

"I almost feel we are," I told her. "I'm sure it was you I saw when I first started shopping here. It must have been about… Well… Janet was three, so forty years ago. You, if it was you, have a daughter about the same age?"

"Yes, I do! I've noticed you too and thought perhaps we could be friends. There wasn't time back then, was there?"

"No. I have time now though." I told her about the shopping list she'd once dropped and the interest I'd developed in learning what people bought and guessing why.

"You must have wondered about that then?" Sue indicated the bag at her feet.

I nodded. I was convinced by then that my initial guess had been wrong.

"Want to come with me and find out?" she suggested.

I did, but my car was parked outside, I'd bought food that

needed to go in the fridge and I didn't know anything about the woman. My hesitation must have shown.

"Sorry, a bit out the blue when we've only just met. It's just that I really do have to go now and I think you might enjoy this afternoon, plus I'd like us to be friends."

"I'd like that too. My car's outside though ..." I explained.

"Of course. Well I'm going to that little hall in Church Street. I'll be there from two until five. Join me if you want to, but if not how about we meet here next week, a bit earlier so we have longer to talk?"

"You've got me curious now and I live close to Church Street. I could walk down."

"I'll be walking too. See you in half an hour or so then," Sue said.

I just had time to put my shopping away, tidy myself up a little and walk to the hall for two o'clock. When I arrived, Sue greeted me and offered me a glass of wine before introducing me to the rest of her flower arranging group.

"I don't know anything about flower arranging," I admitted.

"Neither do most of us really, but Mo is trying to teach us the basics. Really it's just an excuse to get together, chat and drink wine."

"That explains half of your shopping basket," I said.

"The rest is because I heard they help cut flowers last longer. I brought them along to ask Mo."

Mo examined my new friend's purchases, which I realised weren't exactly as I'd first thought. As well as the painkillers I'd seen, there were vitamin C and water purification tablets.

"The vitamin C might help," Mo said. "A squeeze of lemon juice and teaspoon of sugar are what I use. Some people add a drop of bleach, but I don't. It's easy to use too much and kill rather than cure."

I'd like to say I helped Sue with her arrangement that afternoon, but in truth I think I was more of a hindrance. We did have a lot of fun though. I still like to look at other people's shopping lists, but I enjoy my new hobby of flower arranging and my new friendship even more.

15. Awkward Arrangement

"I'm just fed up, Neil, that's all," Cheryl said in answer to her friend's query.

"With what? Work?"

How could she explain? Even her weekly Saturday morning coffee with him irritated her. They'd started it a year ago, after they'd got divorced around the same time. Not once had Cheryl cancelled because she had something better to do.

"I'm bored," she confessed.

"Perhaps you need a hobby? Flower arranging perhaps. You like flowers, don't you?"

"Yes, but Mum's a keen flower arranger. I'm not ready to turn into my mother just yet." Cheryl took another sip of already too cool cappuccino.

"We could do something together this afternoon. Just let me call and cancel …"

"No!" She didn't want to inconvenience him just because she was feeling sorry for herself. "I've got something planned for this afternoon."

"That's good." Neil didn't look relieved, but then he was too polite for that.

They finished their drinks and parted, promising to see each other at work on Monday.

Cheryl's only plan was buying a birthday gift for another friend and colleague, Kath. Even Cheryl's gift buying was in a rut. Nowadays it was a huge box of handmade truffles but she still just gave her best friend chocolates.

"I like chocolates, Cheryl," Kath said last year, when Cheryl apologised for her lack of imagination. "All our money goes on the kids so I …"

"If you need money …"

"I don't. Honestly we have everything we need. It's nice though to have something a bit frivolous, just for me."

As Cheryl headed to the confectioners, she noticed the old bookstore had re-opened as a florist's. Flowers would make a frivolous gift just for Kath.

"Hello," a deep voice greeted Cheryl as she walked into Greg and Sons. An attractive face emerged from behind an enormous fern. The man's manner was as charming as his appearance. He chatted pleasantly as she dithered over her choice.

"What colour bow do you think your friend would like?" he indicated a large selection.

"Oh dear another decision!" Cheryl joked.

"Yellow is cheerful and tones well with the sunflowers."

Cheryl was happy to agree.

"Would you like them delivered?"

"Thank you but I'll take them to her. If you could wrap them or something?"

"I'll do whatever you like." He made a large complicated looking bow, split ribbons and curled streamers until the bouquet was quite spectacular. "There you go, nearly as pretty as you!" The wink which accompanied his salesman's patter made Cheryl grin.

After that all her female friends and relations received

bouquets for their birthdays. Soon Cheryl started buying flowers for herself too. Why shouldn't she have colour and fragrance in her life? And why shouldn't she enjoy a very mild flirtation with Greg the florist if she felt like it? She wasn't deluding herself it meant anything. Even if he'd actually been interested, he was a family man.

On her own birthday Cheryl was given flowers at work as she liked them so much. It was lovely to see her flat bright and cheerful, almost like a florist shop. That illusion was enhanced when Greg delivered yet more flowers that evening.

"Happy birthday!" he said from behind an enormous foil balloon decorated with those same words.

"How did you know?" she laughed.

He shrugged and gave another of his cheeky winks. "This is my last delivery today. I was wondering …"

He never got to say what he wondered as Kath arrived to take her out. It wasn't until the following day Cheryl realised she had more bunches of flowers than cards. Maybe Greg added more because she was such a good customer?

The next time she visited the florist she mentioned the extra flowers and tried to thank him.

"No, Cheryl I didn't give you flowers because you're a good customer. Where would I be if I gave all my flowers away to customers, eh?"

She felt herself blush. Why on earth had she mentioned such a silly idea?

"I wouldn't give them away to just anyone." He presented a little bunch of freesias, sprig of gypsophila and another wink.

As Cheryl tried to explain it wasn't a hint she became

tongue tied. She didn't go back for several days. Not until the flowers and their delicious scent had faded.

For her mum's birthday Cheryl bought a huge foliage pot plant from Greg and Sons. She might not have returned there if Mum hadn't said that was exactly what she'd like. Greg wrapped the plant beautifully, giving advice on its care and no sign he'd been offended by her mistake.

Cheryl was remembering Greg's infectious grin as she arrived at work.

"You look happy," Neil remarked.

"I suppose I am." She hadn't seen Neil smile much lately. He was a lovely man who deserved to be happy. He used to love painting flowers. He'd stopped because his ex wife complained about the mess of the oil paints. If he took up his hobby again it might lift his mood. That gave Cheryl a perfect excuse to return to Greg and Sons.

"I'd like flowers for painting," she told Greg.

"How about these eryngiums?" Greg suggested. "Unusual texture and interesting shapes. You could mix in something softer for contrast."

They picked out deep burgundy stocks which looked wonderful against the silvery eryngiums. Belatedly Cheryl wondered if giving them to Neil might suggest she wanted a change in their relationship. "Could you deliver them anonymously?" she asked Greg.

"No problem."

On Monday, Neil said, "The strangest thing happened. A bunch of flowers was delivered to me by mistake. They were just so perfect for painting I got my oils and worked all weekend. Then on Sunday I popped next door to borrow something and saw a wedding anniversary card from her to him, but there was nothing from him to her. I realised what had happened and gestured for him to follow me. The relief on his face when he saw them! She must have thought he'd forgotten and not been best pleased."

"I just bet she wasn't," Cheryl laughed. "So you're back painting again?"

"I am and I shan't give it up again."

It didn't matter that Neil was unaware they really had been intended for him, as they'd done the job she'd bought them for – and apparently made two other people happy as well.

Neil's renewed enthusiasm for his painting made Cheryl wonder if he was right and she should find a hobby herself. Perhaps the library would have a book on flower arranging. Drat it, why did her thoughts turn to floristry whenever she felt lonely?

On Valentine's Day, a Sunday, Cheryl received a beautiful bouquet of lilies and ferns. She loved the colours and scent but even more she enjoyed Greg delivering them and stopping to chat for a few minutes. It took her quite a while to wonder who'd sent them and why.

A couple of weeks later a bouquet arrived for her at work. Neil noticed, it would have been impossible not to. She'd wondered if they were from him, but he seemed as puzzled as her by the lack of card.

"Who's the mystery man then?" Kath asked.

"No idea," Cheryl said.

She went to Greg and Sons on her way home and asked who'd sent the flowers. "It makes me feel uncomfortable not to know."

"I'm sorry about that. I can explain and ask him not to stop, but I can't tell you who it is."

"No, I suppose you can't if they were ordered in confidence." She sighed. "It doesn't make sense. Why would anyone send flowers but not say who they were from?"

"It's a bit awkward if you're in a relationship with someone else."

"But I'm not."

"Mr Harris?"

"Neil? We're just friends."

"And there's no reason for a man who likes you not to send you flowers?"

"None. But I'd like to know who it is. Well, assuming he's single himself and not weird or anything."

"Righto."

She'd not been home long when her doorbell rang. It was Greg, at least it looked like his hands and feet. That's all that was visible behind the huge quantity of flowers. There couldn't be many left in the shop.

"There's a card this time, if you can find it," he said.

She invited him in. He stood patiently as she took bunch after bunch and put them in vases and jugs and saucepans and the mixing bowl. The card was attached to the very last bunch.

"I don't understand," she said as she stared at Greg's business card.

"I'd have thought it was clear enough. Not so sure about the not weird part, but I am single."

"But it's Greg and Sons."

"I'm one of the sons. Dad's got a shop in Romsey and my brother has one in Petersfield."

"Oh."

A slithering sound, followed by a wet thud, told her the mixing bowl wasn't working very well as a flower vase. It was a shame the petals were bruised but picking them up gave her a chance to gather her thoughts.

"You know I was thinking of taking up flower arranging. I've got everything I need to start now," she said.

"Not everything. You'll need foam and better vases," he tapped the mixing bowl. "I have plenty in the shop. I could bring you some when I collect you to take you to dinner this evening if you like?"

"I'd like that very much."

16. Lily Of The Valley

Hilary Williams scowled. Why couldn't that awful boy keep his window shut when he played his terrible music? She didn't want to hear it any more than she wanted the lily of the valley invading from his parents' garden. The plant was the reason she was freezing cold, struggling to get a fork into the narrow strip of ground between the two houses.

Her previous neighbours, the Greens said they grew it for the lovely scent, but Hilary hadn't noticed any perfume. It was neither use nor ornament!

Gosh, she'd become a misery since retirement. She used to believe there was good in everyone if you looked for it. Hadn't she badgered her own parents about intolerance when they'd had a new family doctor with a very un-English name. Mum wanted to change without even meeting the woman. Hilary said prejudice like that had allowed Hitler to get away with the terrible things he'd done. That shook them and Mum agreed to give the doctor a chance – and found her to be excellent.

Even so, when someone in the street reported they didn't like the sound of Hilary's new neighbours, she'd immediately taken against them.

"Polish they are," the gossip said. "And you know what the papers say about them."

"A lot of unjustified rubbish," is what Hilary should have said, but she'd nodded.

"Apparently they bullied the Greens into accepting a very low offer."

The Greens were wonderful neighbours. They and Hilary took in deliveries for each other and held spare keys. Occasionally they'd invited her for a meal or day out. Hilary was truly sorry when they explained they were moving nearer their daughter.

They'd given Hilary their new address. "Don't forget us once you've made friends with the new neighbours."

Nothing the Greens said hinted the Dubickis were unpleasant in any way.

Hilary gave herself a talking to and offered tea as soon as the removal lorry left. Mrs Dubicki was a teacher. The husband was something to do with computers. They were both very pleasant.

The boy looked a mess with ripped jeans and hair in need of a trim. He'd just nodded at her and disappeared upstairs with a box. He never seemed to do anything except listen to music and hang out of his bedroom window. Hilary found him increasingly annoying. He always came and went via the side passage and usually left the gate open so it banged in the wind. It didn't seem like much, certainly not enough to complain to his parents, but it was irritating.

Just like the lily of the valley. Hilary couldn't exactly blame the Dubickis as the plant had been creeping under the low fence for years. Before the Greens moved, Hilary had almost decided to let it stay. Nothing else grew in that shady strip between the houses. All she really had against it was the lack of promised scent. Just as all she had against the Dubickis was that they weren't the Greens. And their son was a slouching, sullen looking boy, nothing like the Green's daughter who'd always called a cheery greeting.

Hilary hadn't needed to look for good in the Greens; it was obvious. She'd not made the effort for their flowers. Maybe she needed to get close to smell them. Carefully Hilary lowered herself to her knees and bent her head. All she got for her trouble was damp patches on her trousers. To help haul herself up, Hilary clutched the top of the fence. She heaved and heard a crack.

After a moment's panic she realised it was wood which had given away, not her shoulder. She wasn't injured, but she was stuck. The boy's music blared out, proving he was still up in his room. If only he'd go out he'd surely see or hear her as he passed, and fetch help. At last she was willing to look for the good in him and sure she'd find it if she could alert him to her trouble.

Lying on the ground as she was, the boy wouldn't see if she waved. Her garden fork was out of reach. All she had was lily of the valley. Hilary picked flowers and leaves and threw them over the fence.

The music stopped.

"Mrs Williams?"

Hilary threw another flower stem.

"Stay still. I'm coming!"

He might slouch about most of the time, but he was very quick in reaching her.

"Are you hurt?" He sounded really concerned.

"I don't think so. If you could just help me up?"

He did and helped her walk inside. She'd expected that, but was surprised he offered to call a taxi and accompany her to the doctor. When she refused he switched on her electric fire and made tea. His hair was still a mess and rescuing her had made his already scruffy jeans look even worse, but she saw past that at last.

There was a bang from the gate as it crashed against the wall of her house. This time Hilary didn't mind that he'd not stopped to shut it properly.

"Sounds like the rest of the fence has come down," the boy said.

Hilary explained.

"I'll shut it and make sure the fence is OK so it doesn't fall on Mum when she comes home."

He returned with lily of the valley in a glass of water and placed it next to her empty tea cup. "They're just the ones you picked," he said when she thanked him. "Shall I make more tea?"

"Please, and help yourself to chocolate cake from the tin on top of the fridge."

"Home made?"

"Yes."

"Wicked!"

Hilary smiled at his departing back and then sniffed. She sniffed again. Thanks to the warmth of the house there was a strong, sweet scent drifting up from the lily of the valley. Hilary studied the fresh green leaves and the perfect, tiny white bells on the flower stem. They were really quite beautiful if you bothered to look.

17. A Little Rain Must Fall

<u>Maria</u>

The church is booked. Invitations, trimmed with ribbon matching the bridesmaids' dresses, have all been accepted. I'm excited about how many of the items from our wedding list have been promised. The bridal bouquet, six bridesmaid posies, corsages for the mothers, and a dozen buttonholes are ordered. We've tasted the wedding breakfast, evening buffet, champagne for toasts and wine to accompany the meal. I've checked the table decorations match the bridesmaids' dresses and groomsmen's cravats. It's all going to be perfect.

All I have to do now is stick to my diet and hope it doesn't rain. I'll just die it if rains; it would ruin everything.

<u>Amari</u>

Please let it rain. Everything will be OK then. The grain will swell, crops grow and we'll be able to eat. Rain produces sweet grass so the goats give rich, nourishing milk. Perhaps we'd even have enough to sell, so I can buy cloth for my wedding dress.

Fresh water in the well will allow us to clean our homes, our clothes, ourselves. We'll stay healthy. We will live if it rains. I'll get wed if I live.

If the rains don't come in the next month we'll see withered fruit drop from the trees and stunted crops blown away with the dust. We'll sell our books and furniture, the beginnings of our new home, to pay for food.

I watch a tear fall onto the dry earth. I don't let another follow it. Please let it rain.

Maria

The forecast says it might rain on my wedding day. I can't help crying.

Dad hugs me. "A little rain's not the end of the world," he says. "The top can be put up on the car we've hired. I'll ask the people erecting the marquee to close the side panels and you and Dan can look round for nice places inside that'd make good backdrops for your photos."

"I suppose you're right." I hope he is. It's too late to change the date.

"What's up, love? Just the weather or something else?"

"The rain's enough isn't it? What'll Dan's family think if I arrive bedraggled and the reception is a washout? They don't like me much as it is."

"They will when they get to know you, love. Wedding nerves might be hiding your best qualities."

It's not just for Dan's family I want it to go perfectly. Mum and Dad had a quick wedding because his regiment was ordered to Northern Ireland. Mum wore a hastily altered, borrowed dress and the reception was in a pub. They say they didn't mind and it's the years afterwards which matter, but they set up a savings scheme for mine so I know they want a big fancy do this time.

Please don't let it rain.

In The Garden Air

<u>Amari</u>

I heard Fadil singing before I saw him today. He sings of the rain that's coming. Coming very soon according to his grandfather. I've never heard that man tell a lie.

I join Fadil's singing as we help prepare for the rain. We clear ditches to channel it to our families' wilting crops. Fadil climbs up to check the roofs on the grain store and barn. If we're lucky enough to have food to store we'll not let it grow mouldy and rank.

We bring in anything which the rain could spoil. How strange to think that which will make everything right can damage a book of poetry, a rack of drying figs.

It will come, I'm sure of it. The animals are restless and I smell moisture on the air.

<u>Maria</u>

When the cars arrive the bridesmaids and Mum dash out as the first fat drops fall. The driver of my car holds a huge umbrella, in totally the wrong shade, over Dad and I.

"Text the photographer and make sure it doesn't appear in any of the pictures," I instruct Dad. It hardly matters. The whole day is spoiled. Walking up the tree-lined gravel path to the church will make my dress filthy, the open air dance floor will have to go into the marquee making it cramped, and angry tears are threatening to smear my makeup.

"There's a message!" Dad says.

"Ignore it and call the photographer."

"I'd better not, it's from Dan's best man." He reads then asks our driver to pull over.

"What's happened?" I demand.

Dad doesn't want to tell me but I insist. "There was an accident. They're waiting for an ambulance."

Amari

The rains have come! Huge fat drops, sending up clouds of red dust as they land. Soon small streams run everywhere. What music it makes as it gurgles through the ditches we've made and bounces off the tin roof.

Fadil spins me round as we laugh and dance in the rain. We sit when we're dizzy and talk of the feast we shall have on our wedding day. I'm sure I see the vegetables swell as Fadil describes fat golden pumpkins and corn. I smell the meats roasting and feel the sharp tang of cheese in my mouth. The rain washes my face clean of the melon juice that my imagination is trickling down my neck.

There will be enough food for everyone on our wedding day. Our union will be blessed by the joy of our family, friends and neighbours.

Maria

Oh, Dan my love, please be OK. But perhaps it's another member of the wedding party who needs help? They'd wait for any of them. I try to think of something non life-threatening that could need an ambulance. I don't mind the delay, not really, not if everyone is OK.

"Here, take this."

I look up to see the driver offering me a pack of tissues.

"Your makeup will smudge if you're not careful."

"What does that matter?"

"All brides want to look perfect on their wedding day." He

angles his rearview mirror for me.

"And are they all as irritable as me?"

"No. You're by far the worst."

Somehow that steadies me. If it isn't Dan who is hurt then most likely it is someone travelling with him so someone close and he'll need me to be strong, to comfort him, not need attention myself. I tidy myself up as Dad passes on the news of the delay.

Amari

Our wedding day at last. There's no sign now of rain in the sky, but its effects are visible all around. The smiling faces of our guests are healthy, flowers bloom everywhere and tables bend under the weight of food prepared for the feast. It's the most perfect day and I'm perfectly happy.

Maria

"Dan's fine, love. There was an accident but it wasn't his car."

I breathe a huge sigh and hug Dad. Soon I'll be able to hug Dan too. I want to get out the car and dance in the rain.

"What's happened then?" I ask.

I learn a cyclist had been knocked off her bike right in front of their car. The driver called for help, the best man and Dan gave first aid. That included covering her with Dan's long-tailed jacket, which is ruined.

Dan is OK and will be there to marry me. Our friends and family will be there to share in our special day. Those are the things which matter, not the colour scheme or if I arrive at the church with mud on the hem of my dress.

Dad says, "Dan can borrow my jacket for the photos, good thing they're the same even if mine is shorter."

Our wedding starts late, thunder rumbles during the service, we leave church under a rainbow of gaudy umbrellas and confetti sticks to everything. The pathway to the pretty bandstand we'd selected as a photography spot is under water so we have Wellington boots as well as the wrong colour umbrellas in the photos.

Dad's speech is interrupted by a call as he forgot to switch his phone back to silent. It's a message to say the cyclist is coming round after her operation and expected to be fine, so Dad adds that in. His speech gets way too long with far too many toasts. The marquee is packed and, though it doesn't leak, the rising humidity results in drops of condensation splashing down as the evening goes on.

My new husband whispers, "I love you," in my ear.

I'm perfectly happy. It's been the most perfect day; the rain didn't spoil a thing.

18. Breaking With Routine

Although it was some way off our usual time to stop for tea I became aware that mine was the only keyboard clacking away. I looked up to see my colleagues surrounding my desk. Everyone was holding something; a card, flowers, wrapped gift or cake.

"Well, this is a surprise!" I laughed as I said it.

They've been talking about my retirement for weeks and they're a nice bunch so I had expected them to do something to mark the occasion. I've been lucky, I know, to have always worked in pleasant places and with likeable people. Nowhere has been better than the situation I'd held for the previous twelve years. It was time for me to retire though and I was looking forward to the change, despite what some people seemed to think.

I gave up all attempts to work as an array of baked goodies was spread across my work surface. Cakes are something of a tradition in the office. We don't need much excuse for those. We have them every birthday, payday or contrived anniversary. The boss once bought everyone a doughnut because our office chairs were three years old, although it being a miserable, grey Monday may have been a contributing factor. She's a lovely lady, Jennie, very caring. She had a little chat with me asking if there was anything she could do to help me adapt to retirement, but I assured her I was fully prepared for it.

Jennie said a few words to everyone gathered around my

desk, thanking me for my years of service and meticulous time keeping. There were grins and nodded heads at that. I smiled back. I know my careful punctuality really is appreciated even if some of the younger ones do find it amusing.

She handed me the flowers, prettily wrapped package, and card. "Just a little something for you to remember us by, Primrose."

"Thank you." I placed the flowers and gift on my desk and opened the envelope.

"Speech, speech," called someone.

"All in good time," I said. That got a laugh.

I pulled out the card. It was gorgeous. Hand made with pressed flowers, including primroses of course. Everyone had written in it. Not just 'best wishes' and a signature I don't mean, but actually written something. There were poems; some moving, some a little cheeky. There were remembrances of pleasant or amusing things which had happened during my working life and thanks from staff I'd trained. I read them all out, playing for time.

"There's these too," I was handed three tiny canvas bags each containing a potted primrose of a different colour. "I expect you already have lots, but these were so sweet we couldn't resist."

"You can never have too much of a good thing," I assured them, before opening the wrapped gift. Thankfully it wasn't the right shape or weight to be a clock as although I'd treasure it as a memento I already had sufficient, perfectly accurate, clocks.

I was careful with the paper; good quality and printed with primroses. Far too nice to throw away. Inside was the most lovely notebook. It matched the card with its cover design of pressed flowers. The pages inside were as velvety as petals. It would be such a pleasure to write in. There was a pen too, a proper fountain pen in primrose yellow.

"These are just lovely, thank you so much."

They seemed to be waiting for something. After a moment I spotted it, a plain envelope was tucked inside the cover. Inside were garden centre vouchers, a ridiculously generous quantity of them.

"Thank you," I said several times before giving in to their demands for a speech. I told them what they already knew, that they were a wonderful group whose friendship I valued, that although I'd miss my job I was looking forward to my retirement and to writing the book on the history of primroses that I'd been researching for years. As I spoke I kept my attention on the time and at eleven I stopped and declared it was exactly time for our tea break. That got another little laugh before we started on the cakes.

A little later I returned from the lavatory to find myself being discussed. Someone was saying how nice it was that I had an interest to occupy me in my retirement.

"It is, because heaven knows what she'll do without the routine of the office," a friend replied.

"Oh don't worry about me, girls," I said. "I'm looking forward to a complete break from routine."

They didn't look convinced.

I remembered that the following morning and every morning that week as, even without setting the alarm, I awoke at my usual time. I told myself there was no need to get up, I was free from the need to stick to my careful routine. Freedom is choice though and I didn't have to stay in bed either.

Oh OK, I admit it. I've been retired three months now and every morning I get up at the same time as I always have. Instead of driving to work I walk around my garden and then I sit at my desk and begin work at nine exactly. I stop at one for lunch and return to my desk until five. Saturdays are still when I do my main grocery shopping. I still buy or make myself a cake on the last Thursday of the month and any other time I can persuade myself there's a reason to.

Why not? I'm happy. And don't go thinking I'm stuck in a rut. Some days I work away from home, in the library, RHS gardens or at nurseries which stock primroses. I always take my lovely new pen and notebook with me, to record anything I learn. Even when at home I vary my routine. Yesterday I had my morning tea break at ten fifteen and this afternoon I've taken two, both of which I enjoyed in the garden and I've stayed out here, barefoot and wearing nothing but a bikini top and shorts as I work. I doubt they'll be introducing that in your office any time soon!

19. In The Pink

"How about you, Trudie?"

"Sorry, what's that?" Trudie had been studying the overtime list and wondering if she could fit in enough hours to pay for the trainers her son wanted. She couldn't, not without leaving him and his sister on their own after school and they were too young for that.

"They've just discovered loads of boxes of chocolate biscuits in the food hall are nearly out of date. With staff discount they're 50p each, so they're going quick. Want me to get you some?"

"Yes please." Trudie dug a pound coin from her purse. She didn't really need a new lipstick.

Before walking down to the school, she put the biscuits where the children would be bound to notice when they came in. Trudie wouldn't let them open them until they'd had their tea and finished their reading, but until then they'd enjoy the anticipation.

Their delight at biting into biscuits which had a thick chocolate coating all the way round, instead of smeared so thinly on top you couldn't taste it, made Trudie grin.

She packed a couple of the biscuits in her husband's sandwich box and took two in for her own lunch break the following day. She was looking forward to them when she overheard a customer chatting to a friend on her mobile about where to have lunch. She didn't seem to like the sound of anywhere much.

"Oh all right, I suppose so," she said eventually.

The customer returned her attention to the important business of shopping and asked Trudie to fetch two pairs of eye wateringly expensive shoes for her to try. The woman took them without a word. After walking up and down in first one pair and then the other she still couldn't decide which would go best with the new dress she'd bought.

"They both look very nice on you and complement the dress. Is the outfit for a formal occasion?"

"Yes, formal and dull."

"Perhaps these would be more suitable?" Trudie indicated the pair she suggested.

"You're probably right, but I'm not sure about the heel." She shrugged. "Oh, I'll just take them both."

Nice to have the money to solve your problems, Trudie thought. No, that wasn't fair. The woman still couldn't decide which she'd wear and apparently wouldn't enjoy doing so anyway. She was spending more money in one go than Trudie had paid for footwear her whole life, but Trudie loved her comfy slippers, the glamorous sandals which did duty for every summer wedding, and her sturdy winter boots. The customer was about to eat an expensive lunch, but obviously wasn't looking forward to it as much as Trudie was to sitting down for her own break. Who was getting the better deal?

She kept telling herself that as she scurried around picking up the shoes and packing materials before entering the sale in the till.

The woman flicked open her wallet, dropping credit and store cards in the appropriate name of Richerton onto the counter. Before she'd selected which to use, her phone rang.

Trudie couldn't help but overhear not only the words of Mrs Richerton, but also some of what the caller, a girl named Sasha, had to say. It seemed that a junior Richerton had chickenpox and must be collected from school. Sasha would do this, but Mrs Richerton would have to arrange for his care afterwards as Sasha was too busy doing something else. Quite what that was, Trudie didn't catch.

"I'll be back in an hour and a half," Mrs Richerton said with even less animation than when she'd made her lunch arrangement. She snapped her phone closed and handed over a credit card. "Honestly, now I suppose I'll have to spend the afternoon organising a nurse or nanny or something."

Trudie wasn't jealous of the other woman now; she was angry. Her son would no doubt be feeling poorly and possibly worried about his spots. Didn't Mrs Richerton want to comfort him? Wasn't his welfare more important than a boring lunch? No amount of money and hired help would stop Trudie being concerned about her children's health. When her two had chickenpox one after the other they were fractious and irritable and no one got much sleep for several weeks. Oh but the bliss when she saw them getting better.

"Oh dear? Is he seriously ill?" Trudie asked, trying hard to keep her voice polite.

"No. That's what makes it worse. What's the point of a boarding school if they don't keep the children?"

"You're annoyed your son isn't seriously sick?"

The customer gasped and glared at Trudie, the first time she'd looked her in the face. That didn't last long though as she soon glanced down to the badge bearing both the store and Trudie's names.

"I'm sorry, madam I shouldn't have said that." Oh what the heck, she'd already made her feelings perfectly plain. "It's just… my own two had it not so long ago. Naturally you'll be worried about your son, but getting a stranger to care for him might alarm him. With mine I found what soothed them most was a lotion you can get at the chemist and just being there."

Mrs Richerton didn't speak again, just pulled her credit card from machine and picked up her bag. She didn't thank Trudie, but then she'd not been expecting any gratitude even before she'd suggested the woman was a heartless mother. She did expect a complaint, but none came. Trudie hoped Mrs Richerton had after all decided not to ignore her son until his absence from school fitted into her demanding schedule of shopping and lunch and was therefore too busy to make trouble for a shop assistant.

She thought she'd put the incident from her mind until Jan, her supervisor, asked for a word during her break the following day.

"Is there a problem?" Trudie asked.

"I hope not, but it's about the lottery money …"

Trudie knew she owed for a couple of weeks, but only because they weren't allowed to carry their own cash on the shop floor and Trudie's breaks hadn't coincided with her supervisor's for some time. "Oh yes, sorry. Here you are." She handed over the money she'd put by.

"Thanks. Oh and how do you feel about switching to women's wear this afternoon? They're a bit short handed."

"I don't mind. It'll make a change."

Winning the lottery would make more of a change, she thought as she made her way to the second floor. All her financial troubles would be over and she wouldn't need to work… She'd miss her part time job though. It wasn't exactly easy but made a break from the chores at home. Though if she won the lottery she wouldn't have to do those. That'd take some getting used to.

Trudie tidied the rails of clothing, ensuring everything was on the correct hanger, arranged according to size, and displayed the correct price label. As she worked she noticed the customers. Some riffled excitedly through the sales racks, sometimes optimistically enquiring if the garment was available at that price in their size.

"It'd look fab at a party I'm going to, but I'd never slim into it on time."

Trudie suggested the tactic she adopted whenever she was invited anywhere. "How about updating something you already have with costume jewellery or a pretty scarf?" She smiled as they looked enthusiastically through the accessories on offer.

Other customers listlessly sifted through the 'new arrivals' taking no pleasure in the luxurious fabrics, or asked advice on what to wear to glamorous events they obviously weren't excited about attending.

"Penny for them?" Jan said.

"I was just thinking that money doesn't make people happy."

"No, but it let's you be miserable in comfort, as my gran used to say."

"I like that!"

"So how about we increase what we pay into the lottery syndicate? Double our chances?"

That meant over £100 a year on something they probably wouldn't win and which might not bring any happiness if they did. "I'd rather not."

"You're not the only one, but a few others like the idea. I was thinking we could do our own lottery and have a monthly prize of £50. The odds of winning would be loads better."

"If you can talk everyone else round, then I'm in."

Trudie imagined being the first winner. She could take the children out for the day and not have to keep saying no to ice creams. They could all go to the pictures, or she could put it towards the ballet lessons her daughter wanted. She certainly wouldn't spend it in the shop. Not that they didn't sell some lovely things, but things didn't really make a person happy, she'd seen that. She approached the till, thinking she'd start persuading the girl there to accept Jan's lottery scheme. As she approached, the phone rang.

"Hello Mrs Richerton… oh dear, I'm sorry to hear that… I'll just get her for you."

Trudie, assuming what the girl was sorry to hear was a complaint about Trudie's rudeness and 'her' was Jan, considered pouncing on the phone and pleading with Mrs Richerton not to speak to the supervisor. After all, could she make things any worse?

"Mrs Richerton has something to ask you," the other assistant said.

Surprised, Trudie took the phone and gave her name.

Mrs Richerton sounded quite frantic. "It's about the ointment …the school sent him home with calamine lotion. Is that what you used?"

"Yes. It does help but the spots will still itch. I put mittens on to stop them scratching."

"He wouldn't sleep. Is that normal?"

"Afraid so."

She asked more questions and as Trudie did her best to advise and reassurance, Mrs Richerton spoke more calmly. "I'm sorry to have bothered you but no one I know has nursed a child through this."

No they've had the staff do it, Trudie thought. Had she shocked Mrs Richerton into doing it herself?

"And I'm not used to going without sleep."

Trudie could easily sympathise with that. "Do contact your doctor if you're worried, but it sounds just the same as when mine had it. I'm sure your boy will be fine."

Two weeks later Trudie was called down to the floristry department. "A Mrs Richerton has ordered flowers for you. Would you like to choose them?"

Trudie was given a dictated note thanking her for the advice and saying the boy was much better.

"I'd like some freesias, they smell so nice," Trudie said.

The florist selected a nice fat bunch. "Now, what else?"

Trudie almost said the freesias were enough on their own, then spotted the delicate pink rosebuds. Horribly expensive, but Mrs Richerton could afford them and they were so very pretty.

The florist must have followed her gaze as he said, "They'd be appropriate."

"How do you mean?"

"Pink roses are said to symbolise gratitude, thankfulness and joy."

"I'll have six then, please."

"You can have a couple of dozen if you like. She said you're to have £100 worth."

"That's madness. What a complete waste of money, no

offence. Just charge her for six …and the freesias."

"Too late, she paid over the phone. Look, I can't give you the rest in cash, but I can give you store gift vouchers."

As Trudie picked out a smart shirt for her husband, spangly head band for her daughter and dinosaur book for son she imagined their reactions. Then she thought of the timing of Mrs Richerton's gift. It hadn't come after Trudie's few words of advice, so wasn't in gratitude for Trudie's help. It came after the child recovered and suggested the mother's relief was so great she'd wanted to share her joy. That thought pleased Trudie just as much as the bag full of nice things she was taking home.

20. All About Her

Listening to the check-out girl tell me the total that Friday was even worse than usual. I just didn't have the money and had to ask her to cancel some items. Was that to be my life from then on? One disappointment after the next? The worst part was it hurt the kids. The expensive cereal they liked had to go and the little treats I'd planned to slip into their lunch boxes. They didn't have much to smile about lately, didn't they at least deserve some chocolate and a pack of stickers?

"Don't worry, it often happens," the check-out girl said. She pressed her buzzer and briefly explained to her supervisor. There seemed to be a procedure in place so at least I didn't have the added indignity of putting the items back on the shelves. That made me feel worse for feeling sorry for myself when so many other people were in the same difficulties. I still had a fairly full trolley; we wouldn't go hungry. Some people needed food banks just to keep going. Things could be a lot worse.

And then they were. I spotted my loud mouthed colleague Teresa in the growing queue. Tales of my woes would be all over the office Monday morning. Teresa's basket wasn't full of own label essentials of course. She didn't have hungry kids to feed or a tight budget. I was surprised she was shopping at all. A few hours earlier she'd been bragging about DN, that's the office nickname for her dishy neighbour, taking her to Luigi's. I had a horrible feeling the fresh salmon was for her cat! Me and mine would be making do with fish finger sandwiches.

If I was single I'd have spent the evening soaking in a bath, doing my hails, blow drying my hair and all the other things I no longer had time for. Teresa never bothered with any of that. Was it surprising the dishy neighbour had taken so long to ask her out?

Teresa talked non-stop and hijacked every conversation. It reminded her of someone she knew, or something she'd seen or heard and off she'd go gossiping away. And you couldn't help listening. Her stories were often amusing, but more frequently downright hilarious. They were wildly exaggerated of course and rarely complimentary, even when they involved herself. Until recently that hadn't seemed to matter.

My husband left me. Usual thing. He'd fallen for a younger, slimmer prettier girl. I'd felt so betrayed. I'd brought up his children. I put up with his interfering mother and the weekends playing golf even before he met someone else. And the big house far away from play parks and friendly neighbours with kids of their own, because that's what would impress the people he worked with. I'd had to keep working through the break up. Most people were shocked but sympathetic. Teresa rubbed it in with her tales of women so much better off being single. Teresa probably counted herself amongst that lot, but I thought she was covering the fact no man would have her.

We'd had a holiday booked and paid for, Les and I. All inclusive, Caribbean luxury. My sister suggested I take her. I'd been reluctant, but Teresa told some story about a hapless husband trying to look after his kids for a weekend. That persuaded me. We had such a good time I temporarily forgot my problems.

Of course Les didn't meet me at the airport with tears of regret in his eyes and apologies on his lips. I hadn't been counting on that, but had hoped he'd work out it was hard work looking after the kids and holding down a full time job without support. Didn't work. He'd just left them with his mother, which had admittedly been the plan when the two of us were to go together. He'd only seen them for a few hours in the evenings and at weekends. The kids were thoroughly spoiled, so when it was back to reality I seemed mean expecting them to eat vegetables and go to bed at a reasonable time. They'd quickly got used to being driven around again too and the struggle of getting them to the bus stop for school started all over again. How do you explain to six and eight year olds that a five minute delay leaving the house means a missed bus so more than a half hour delay arriving and notes from their teacher and disapproving glances from my boss for me?

At work I'd wanted to put all that behind me and relive the holiday, but every conversation turned into one about a holiday of Teresa's or of someone she knew. Those were all hilarious disasters and my tales of a nice room, nice weather, nice food, couldn't hold anyone's interest although a few people asked out of politeness.

As I'd guessed, when I arrived on the Monday after the shopping ordeal, Teresa had a giggling huddle around her. I could have done with a laugh myself, but the stories aren't funny if you're the butt of the joke. Probably just as well I was late again. Although I hated to be, and risked getting into trouble, I'd missed most of Teresa's bitching.

"You OK, Lotta?" a colleague asked.

"It hasn't been a great weekend." Friday night was just the start. Les had promised to take the children out on Saturday, then cancelled at the last minute.

"As bad as Teresa's?" she interrupted without a word of sympathy.

"What?"

"The tortoise? Didn't you hear? She was helping her neighbour whose tortoise escaped, which you'd think would be easy, but they move faster than you'd think. At one point she was crawling through a hedge after it and showed her knickers to DN and …"

Teresa overheard and gave me the full story. It went on and on. All highly amusing, especially as it seemed to have distracted her from my embarrassment in the supermarket.

At lunch I read Teresa's paper. I couldn't afford one and made do with picking up hers when she'd finished. Usually she left it for anyone who wanted but that time I had to fish it out the bin, which hardly helped my mood. There was a report of someone collapsing in Luigi's on Friday evening. He'd been taken out by his family who'd watched horrified as a waiter and another diner performed CPR. How awful for them. Thankfully they'd revived him. No wonder Teresa hadn't said a word about the boring incident of a woman who couldn't afford her shopping. That was much more exciting. She hadn't said a word about that either though. Had she even been at Luigi's?

She hadn't, had she? She was lying about the date. The dishy neighbour wasn't the slightest bit interested in bitchy Teresa: good for him! That explained her being in the supermarket buying fish. And her not wanting people to see the piece in the paper. All those stories of her trying to catch DN's eye and things going wrong were all lies. Probably everything she'd said was… and I'd allowed myself to get jealous over it all.

"Lotta, can I have a word?" the boss, Kezia, said just as I was wondering what to do about my discovery.

"Is everything OK?" she asked once I was sat in her office.

"Yes, fine." That was as big a lie as Teresa's of course, but I didn't dare admit I was barely coping with full time work and so have my hours cut or lose the job altogether. Les had agreed to me keeping the house and mortgage, but seemed to think that meant he could pay virtually no maintenance.

"The new hours working out all right?" she asked.

"Yes. Well usually. It depends on the busses. I know I've been late a couple of times." A couple of times a week would be more accurate. I was cancelling out Teresa's exaggerations with my understatements. "But I work through lunch to make up the time."

"Yes, I know you do."

I didn't mind doing that. It meant less time listening to Teresa and less time to notice I was chomping my way through whatever was on special offer that week.

"And other than work? Everything OK?"

Oh god, Teresa hadn't kept quiet then, she'd told our boss! Probably suggested she watch the stationery cupboard in case I stole paper for my children to draw on.

Attack seemed a better option than defence. "Teresa tells lies! Look, look at this!" I waved the paper. "If she made that up, why would you believe her about what happened in the supermarket?"

"Perhaps you'd like to tell me yourself?"

I remembered Kezia's kindness after Les left. How she found simple tasks to keep me occupied and employed while I pulled herself together those first few days. How she'd quickly agreed to increase my hours and was always understanding about time off if it were needed for something to do with the children. She wouldn't sack me just because of a few bitchy remarks of Teresa's. Gradually all my worries came flooding out. Kezia was brilliant. She made tea and handed over tissues, then got on the internet and found out about free school meals and the like.

"There's absolutely no shame in asking for help if you need it," she'd said. "Lots of people do. My daughter's children have the free meals since my son-in-law was made redundant."

I remembered what the check-out girl said about me not being the only person unable to pay for a full trolley of groceries. It was true, plenty of people were in a similar position and they, unlike Teresa, wouldn't be judging me.

"I'm no expert in these matters," my boss continued. "How about we get you an appointment with Citizen's Advice and perhaps a lawyer or something to get your maintenance payments properly arranged?"

"Thank you. I should have done all that myself, but I didn't want to admit I had to; that it was all over."

I spent the next few days going from appointment to appointment. Everyone was brilliant, Kezia for allowing me to take the time and brushing it off with a murmur about it being nothing; the various professionals who explained what I was entitled to. Money didn't start flooding in immediately of course, but just knowing some would trickle through enabled me to cope. One advisor suggested I sell the house and buy something smaller. I'd still be left with a mortgage but a far more manageable one. Such an obvious thing to do, but I'd not been thinking straight.

I was in a far more cheerful frame of mind when I did the

shop that Friday. As usual I'd dropped the children off on the way, but once they'd dashed off to play in their grandparents' large garden I'd calmly laid down a few ground rules. I was happy for them to maintain regular contact with my children; it was in everyone's best interests, but if they had them on a school night they were to go to bed at the times I said. If I'd said no to a particular toy, film or TV programme they were to uphold the ban. Just simple little things, but it made me feel in control again. My soon to be ex in-laws readily agreed and it soon became apparent my rules had generally been flouted because they'd been unaware of them. Les, their son, didn't think any rules applied to him and hadn't bothered passing them on. He did however take the children that weekend as he'd promised.

I went home from shopping and shaved my legs, did my nails, blow dried my hair, had a glass of wine. I looked great. It was just a shame there was no one to see it. No, it wasn't really. With relief I realised I was over my ex enough not to wish he could see me looking my best. I wasn't like Teresa, desperate to go to any lengths to attract a man; and boy did she go to some lengths! Maybe it was because I wasn't used to the wine, but I giggled as I remembered her antics. The time she'd decided to show her dishy neighbour how fit she was by setting up swing ball in her garden.

The ball flew off, hitting her in the face and crashing into another neighbour's prized dahlias. Fortunately the elderly gentleman, who had a bit of a reputation as a ladies man, had seen the incident and realised it was an accident. Less fortunately he'd then come round with a bunch of the blooms to show there were no hard feelings. The man was a bit deaf and shouted. DN had looked out and seen Teresa being given flowers and leaning in close to the giver so he could hear her words of thanks. The next day she'd had two black eyes from where the ball had hit her, so hadn't even appealed to ninety-year-olds.

Then there was the time one of the girls at work had a cold sore and had been in a silly state about how it would make her look hideous at a friend's wedding. She was going to be bridesmaid and had a crush on the best man. Teresa had launched into another, rather steamy, story about the bridesmaid and best man at her cousin's wedding. By the time she finished the girl had cheered up enough to stop worrying and picking at her lip and the tiny blemish cleared up long before the big day.

There were other times when Teresa's stories had accidentally done some good. It had happened over my holiday. Teresa's constant interruptions dragged out the conversation so I had longer to relive that happy time. Also some of the stories reminded me Les had been rather selfish in a lot of ways. That had been the beginning of my realisation it as much my pride and bank balance which had taken a knock as my heart, and that in some ways I was better off without him.

I had a whole weekend to do just as I pleased. It was a bit boring really and I knew I'd be glad to have the children back. I started to see why Teresa was so desperate to attract her dishy neighbour and almost felt sorry for her.

Rather than brooding I took myself for a long walk. Who should I spot but Teresa – with a really ugly man. I guessed she'd have something funny to say about him on Monday. It wouldn't be fair though. It wasn't the poor man's fault that his face looked so strange. I had the idea of making up a story about a heroic cousin who got horribly burned rescuing someone from a fire. By the time Teresa started making fun of her companion the ugly man would have everyone's sympathy and Teresa's bitchiness would be obvious. I didn't get the chance.

Les was late bringing back the children because he'd decided to let them watch something on TV which I always said no to. As a result they were late into bed and woke up frightened. After a very disturbed night we were all late at school and work. When I arrived Teresa was telling everyone she'd finally had a date, of sorts, with DN. "Seemed he was a bit shy to ask me out, and who can blame him after the craziness which is my life?"

There were jokey comments about how brave he'd been to even think of it.

"He must really like you."

"Actually it seems he does." She'd gone all gooey eyed. "Who'd have thought it?"

I thought she was rather overdoing it but, not wanting to look bitchy myself, asked where he'd taken her.

"The park, on Sunday. He'd suggested a coffee, but we chatted until lunch time, so had a meal in the pub together and then walked round, still talking, until it was dark. You know how on the films people meet and talk all night and it passes like seconds? It was just like that."

Except it wasn't because I'd seen her with the ugly bloke. Walking in the park was true, but the rest was rubbish. Just like her going to Luigi's with him. I was tempted to expose her, but remembered how lonely her life must be. Could I blame Teresa for wanting to make it sound more interesting? Besides it wasn't just bitchiness, her stories always raised a smile and couldn't we all do with more of that?

"Hang on, Teresa. This wasn't your first date!" someone said. "Didn't he take you to Luigi's?"

"Oh, don't talk about Luigi's!"

"Come on, tell us!"

Teresa tried to change the subject, but for the first time ever, wasn't able to.

"Well, you remember the exploding jam incident?"

There was laughter as that catastrophe was recalled, but everyone wanted to know how it was relevant.

"Well, the lady in question hasn't been too well and not wanting to spoil the evening worrying about her, or having DN ask after her and think me heartless for not knowing, I called in. Poor dear hadn't any decent food in the house, so I nipped down the shop and got her a bit of fish. She's the traditional type. Did I tell you about the time she …"

"Don't change the subject, Teresa!" someone said.

"Oh, well I was sure she'd be tempted by fish on a Friday. She was, so I quickly cooked it up for her and took the skin home for Fluffy. Never get a cat if you want a date, I'm telling you! Rather than be properly grateful and eat it there and then the rotten hairball carried it off to my bedroom. The bedroom in which the drop dead gorgeous dress with which I was to wow DN was laid out. Took me ages to get the cat hairs off, but there was nothing I could do about the smell."

"Febreze would have done it."

"It would indeed. Had I used that all would have been well, but I grabbed WD40 instead."

"What's that when it's at home?"

"A lubricant spray to stop hinges squeaking and free up engine parts," I explained.

"Exactly," Teresa said. "So I arrived late, smelly fishy and as though I'd been snogging a mechanic. Still, at least I was well lubricated!"

She got her usual laugh and by then we'd had quite a long break so she was spared, temporarily at least, explaining what happened when she got to Luigi's, if she ever did. I realised that when I'd wondered why she wasn't home preening, she'd been helping a neighbour in need. The next weekend I'd spent pampering myself, even though I have an elderly neighbour who, come to think of it, I hadn't seen for a few days. I made a mental note to check on her that evening and to try to be less judgemental about Teresa too. A lot of her disaster stories started out with her trying to do someone a good turn, although that part was glossed over in the over-egged parts about how badly it turned out.

That lunchtime Teresa sat quite near me in the canteen. I was still feeling slightly abashed and didn't want to talk to her. I rummaged in my bag, intending to look busy on my phone and found the newspaper I'd been reading when I'd been called in to Kezia's office and she'd put me on track to sorting my life out. Someone must have tipped her off about my difficulties and that someone was almost certainly Teresa. She hadn't kept her mouth shut as I'd thought, she'd quietly told the person who needed to know, but not mentioned it to anyone else.

I looked again at the piece about Luigi's. I hadn't read it all before jumping to the conclusion Teresa was a liar. Maybe I'd got the date wrong or something. The dates was right and so was her story. She'd been there because she was the customer performing CPR. She'd saved the man's life. That was a huge story, but she'd not said a word. I guessed the paper had gone in the bin that day so as to keep it quiet. She'd kept quiet when that's what I'd wanted, if she didn't want this to get out I wouldn't say anything… I had to know though, why she didn't tell us.

I slid the paper towards her and when she glanced at it, tapped the article.

"Oh."

"Why didn't you say?" I asked.

"It wasn't my story."

"Of course it was, you saved his life."

"I'm a first aider with St John's ambulance. I was just doing what I was trained to do. For me it wasn't a big deal, but can you imagine what it was like for that poor man's family?"

"They must be really grateful to you."

"Should think they'd rather forget I exist and that the whole thing ever happened. I would if I was them. He's local, so if I talked about it then it might get back to them and remind them of watching helpless as his lips went blue and I, well you know."

I didn't because I'd have watched helplessly, not rushed to help. "You're a hero."

"Nah, you know me. I just like to be the centre of attention. That's why I joined St John's. Usually we go to village fetes and the like. The things people do to themselves! One time the mayor was judging a fancy dress competition. One kid was done up like a tiger, or a dragon or something and was picked out as one of the final three. He was so excited he got into character and bit the mayor."

Dog or dragon or something? If he was in the top three she'd have been able to work out what he'd come as. My kids had taken part in a few fancy dress competitions and the youngest was likely to get over excited. He's never bitten the judge, but if he had no one would have recognised him from the story. No one was ever recognisable in her stories as being in the wrong or the figure of fun unless it was Teresa herself.

"So what about your dishy neighbour? Are you happy to talk about him?"

"Too happy to, I'm afraid. I don't want to bore everyone, but I'm like teenager with a mad crush. You know thinking about him all the time and doodling his name when I should be working."

"Oh yes, I remember what that was like! It's been a while, but I remember."

"Oh god! I'm sorry, I didn't think."

"It's OK. Not all relationships go horribly wrong and I really, really hope yours doesn't."

"Thank you."

"So go on, tell me about him."

"Well, like I've said lots and lots of times, I've liked him for ages and tried to sort of encourage him, but he's shy. Well not shy exactly. Self conscious is maybe a better word. He's not that confident when it comes to women. He should be though. You mentioned heroes, he really is one. There was a fire and he rescued a family despite being hurt himself."

"Ah that explains …"

"Explains what?"

"I saw you. In the park on Sunday."

"Oh. Right."

"He has a lovely smile and a really sexy laugh."

"Oh yes, doesn't he?"

Her stories of the developing romance between her and DN didn't bore us at all, but I could tell Teresa was growing uncomfortable with the increasing requests to meet him, or at least see a picture. When that happened I interrupted and told everyone about the time my third cousin's next door neighbour doctored his wedding pictures and put a hippo on his mother-in-law's head and she saw it. Teresa and I, who'd become close friends by then, would regularly exchange a wink and take the conversation away on mad twists and turns.

"I should stop talking rubbish," she said one day just after that had happened. "I've built DN up so much that people will be shocked when they see him."

I shook my head.

"Are you saying you weren't?"

"OK, I was a bit… but it's just an initial impression. I hardly notice the scars now. Actually I think they're fading." That was true.

"So do I, but you know I'm right. He wants to meet my other friends and if I keep saying no it looks like I'm ashamed of him."

"Come on, no one who's heard you talking about him could think that."

"That's the trouble. It'll be a shock and they won't be able to help him seeing that. It'd really knock his confidence."

"I understand, but the longer you put it off the worse it'll be."

"I suppose."

"Look, bring him to the do on Saturday."

"OK"

"Actually bring him. Not say you will then come in on Monday with a massive disaster story."

Now I could have done what I had with the children before they'd met Teresa's dishy neighbour and explained DN was a really nice person but, you know, not quite as good looking as Teresa's nickname for him suggested. That might have done the trick. It's not much of a story though, is it? So I did some digging and found out about the incident in which he'd got his scars and then had a quiet word with our ever understanding boss. She made sure Teresa was out of the way on Friday when I did my big, "You lot will never guess what I've found out!" bit.

I started off by telling them DN's real name was Dean Noble. "Noble by name and by nature, as it turns out."

I gave them every heroic detail and showed them pictures taken soon after. DN hardly looked human in the worst of them but due to my story and the way Teresa had glowed when she talked about him, everyone saw his inner beauty. So much so that when he arrived Saturday evening, with scars no longer an angry red and that lovely smile on his face, we all saw an attractive man. Well, an attractive couple, because Teresa looked as happy as I've ever seen her and after all it's always all about her.

21. Part Of The Place

Jill paused outside the gates to Solent House and adjusted her shoulder bag. The box nestled safely inside it hadn't seemed particularly heavy when she left home, but had gradually felt more of a burden with each step. It was important that she didn't draw too much attention to what she carried until she was ready. Jill wanted to recall happy memories, not answer awkward questions.

Her husband Martin had always like the Georgian mansion. As a child he'd picnicked in the grounds. Later the gates were padlocked shut, but as a teenager Martin had found a way in and sometimes took Jill with him.

After Solent House was handed over to a conservation trust which restored it, the pair of them had visited together many times. Since his retirement Martin had worked there full time as a volunteer for as long as his health had allowed. It was the right place to scatter his ashes.

Jill bought a ticket and followed the path up towards the house. When she reached the terrace she rested on a bench. The sweep of grass in front of her was kept mown now, but not so tightly cut that meadow flowers couldn't bloom. The clover, yarrow, buttercups and ox-eye daisies she remembered from her illicit visits with Martim were still thriving. Without tall grasses to smother them, dainty harebells and fragrant cowslips, as well as exotic looking wild orchids were also now growing well.

Jill had intended to sprinkle Martin's ashes there, but saw

that wouldn't be possible. Children were playing on the grass. Even if she had the authority to move them on, stopping children from playing wasn't something to involve Martin in. Perhaps a quiet corner would be a better resting place. Where though? She wasn't sure who to ask, or even if she should ask. What if they said no?

"Mrs Kildry?" It was Samuel, who she'd always thought of as Martin's lad, although he was a grown man now.

Jill and Martin had both been saddened they couldn't have children, but dealt with it in different ways. Jill put all her energies into accountancy. Martin worked as a caretaker in a primary school. As well as caring for the building, he'd made props for plays, helped on trips and sports days. He'd loved it.

He'd loved working at Solent House too. Martin's favourite area was the schoolroom. He'd told young visitors about the old toys and lessons the children of the house would once have had. He explained the need for great care around fragile original items and encouraged children to play with replica games and toys. On good days this was done outside.

He'd told her about a young lad who was often hanging around.

"You see a lot of children. It sounds as though there's something different about this one," Jill had said.

"There is. Kids are allowed in free, but they're supposed to have an adult with them and come in through front gate – not over the fence."

"Oh dear. He's trouble then?"

"I don't know. Someone recognised him as being part of a family who've recently moved to the area. It seems they keep getting evicted."

"Definitely trouble then."

"Quite possibly the parents are, but it doesn't follow that Samuel is the same."

"Perhaps not."

Martin had encouraged the boy to join in the play.

"He's not interested in the games so much as the old-fashioned lessons," Martin later told Jill. "I don't think he's been taught to read or write."

Martin had gradually won Samuel's trust and discovered his guess was right. It soon became apparent Samuel had a fairly awful home life and was better off staying away as much as possible. Martin made arrangements that the boy be considered a volunteer, working with him every weekend.

"It's big risk, love," Jill told Martin. "If he gets into trouble you'll lose your place."

"If someone doesn't help him he'll end up like the rest of his family. That's a bigger risk."

Jill had seen Samuel numerous times over the years, usually when she walked down to have afternoon tea at the house with Martin. He'd left school with a few qualifications – and a glowing reference from Martin for a full-time job on the maintenance team at the house.

The lad had come to Martin's funeral, Jill remembered. She'd not spoken to him beyond the 'thank you for coming,' she'd said to everyone. Had hardly looked at him then in fact, but she'd not taken much notice of anything.

There, in the place which had meant so much to her husband, Jill looked up at the young man.

"Mrs Kildry… I'm so sorry about Martin."

She nodded and shook his hand.

"I'm just about to go on my break. Can I get you a cup of tea?"

"Thank you. Would it be possible to have it near the schoolroom? That was Martin's favourite place."

"Mine too, because of him. There's some work going on outside it, so the area is closed off to the public, but I can make an exception for you."

She'd had to put on a hard hat. He'd insisted on that with some authority, just as he had that she be allowed through. The area was rather bleak, but Samuel assured her it would soon be transformed. He'd fetched her tea and they'd talked for a while.

Martin had taken a risk with this young man. Jill did the same and told him about her wish for Martin's ashes to be spread at Solent House.

Samuel looked thoughtful for a moment and then grinned. "I know exactly what to do, but it will take a while. Is that OK?"

She decided it was and gave him the precious parcel. Somehow she felt sure that whatever Samuel did that, in trusting him to help, Jill had done what Martin would have wanted her to.

Months later Samuel telephoned. "The new area outside the schoolroom is being opened soon. I'd like you to come as my guest."

"I'd like that, thank you. Have you... Did you... The box I gave you... ?"

"Oh yes!"

Samuel was right about the area being transformed. What was once a draughty, tatty lawn was now a lovely sheltered courtyard with games for children to play, and a plaque in Martin's memory. A small one tucked away in a corner.

"Perfect," Jill said. "He'd have liked that far more than anything flashy."

"I hope he, and you, will also be pleased with what I did with his ashes."

Samuel confessed he'd mixed them into several batches of cement which were used for the walls and foundations. Martin was literally supporting the chair on which she sat and sheltering her from the wind. For generations to come he would do the same for visiting children.

"Thank you," Jill said. "This place has always been important to him and now he'll be a permanent part of it."

22. A Year In A Garden

<u>January</u>

A splash of bright magenta in the garden caught Ruby's attention. She'd been hunched over her computer all morning and had needed to stretch her legs and breathe fresh air, even if it was cold and damp. She bent down and saw a plant, half covered in sodden dead leaves, was struggling to flower. Ruby cleared away the fallen leaves, revealing a patch of cyclamen coum. Now they were exposed to the light they could flaunt their blooms.

A little splash of brightness was just what she needed. Callum had been particularly dour lately and their relationship was showing strain. It didn't help that he left for work at the bank in the dark and returned in the dark and was inside all day. The only times he saw daylight was the weekends. She'd be miserable too under such conditions. How lucky she was that her job as a freelance graphic designer allowed her to work from home. She was able to get out into the garden for a break during any fine weather. Callum would love to do that too… at least he would have done in the past. Lately he seemed to have as little interest in the garden as he did in anything else. Ruby photographed the cyclamen and printed it out for him to have on his desk, so he didn't miss out entirely.

<u>February</u>

The yellow aconites glowing in their little green ruffs were so pretty and looked fabulous with the snowdrops and very earliest crocus. On sunny days it almost felt like spring. Ruby tried to capture that feeling in a photo for Callum. He needed something to give him hope, what with his worries about work. No one seemed to have a good word to say about bankers these days. If only the reports of big bonuses were as true for the middle managers as well as those at the very top.

Odd to think the plants that cheered the garden in winter vanished by summer and were all but forgotten. Ruby decided to create a calendar showing the garden at its best in each month. They could use it next year when she hoped, just like the aconites, their problems would have withered away to nothing.

March

Ruby captured a lovely image of the jewel-like early iris backlit by spring sunshine. She printed it out for her husband, but it never got displayed on Callum's desk.

"I'll be clearing it soon, so it's silly to take anything else in."

Were things really so bad? Ruby hoped not. If he lost his job they'd lose the house and that meant losing the garden. Callum was probably just being negative. He'd been that way for some time now. But if it wasn't his job, what was making him unhappy? Did he have concerns about his health or the family? Or was it her? Their life together?

April

Tulips always reminded Ruby of their honeymoon in The Netherlands. They'd ordered bulbs for the garden even though it was still a building site at that point. Between them they'd built the garden up from scratch, until they had a patch of ground which was not just spectacular in spring but beautiful in every season. Now it was all falling apart. Not the garden, but everything else.

Every year they'd studied the bulb catalogues together, deciding which tulips to add to their collection, where to plant them and what to follow them with. Ruby couldn't imagine them doing that this year; Callum wouldn't discuss the future. When she handed him the best of her tulip photographs he took it without a word.

May

The dicentra plant had grown into a magnificent clump. Bleeding heart some people called it. Ruby had never liked that name, preferring instead lady-in-the-bath as, by turning the flowers upright and the application of a good dose of imagination, they did resemble that image. Now though Bleeding Heart seemed appropriate; the flowers dripped down like tears. Ruby sat on the soft grass and cried.

Callum came out into the garden for the first time in months. He reached down and placed a hand on her shoulder. "You know?" he asked.

"I know something is wrong, but not what."

"I've been made redundant. I'm due a settlement, but not a big one. Not big enough to keep the house."

"When?"

"I won't be going in again. I get paid for a few weeks, time to help me adjust or look for something else …"

They both knew the chances of his finding alternative employment and at his age were slim.

"They can't just do this. Aren't the unions supposed to be called in and for there to be consultations?"

"They've done all that."

"In three months?"

"No, it started just when you were going self-employed. I didn't say because I didn't want you to worry."

So he'd shouldered it all himself. He'd let her leave her job without knowing all the facts, let her make plans for the garden she'd loose. They were supposed to be a team, to talk to each other. If they couldn't do that, what was the point?

"I should have told you, I know that now. But that would have made it real."

She saw tears fill his eyes. That had only happened once before; when he'd lifted her veil on their wedding day.

"Tell me I'm not too late. That I've not lost you as well."

"It's not too late," she said. "Of course it's not too late."

He pulled her up and into his arms. They talked then, about the garden. They'd created it and created something special between them, they could do it again.

<u>June</u>

Clematis flowers peeped out from every plant strong enough to host them. No, not peeped, that was too subtle a word for such gorgeously bold blooms. They surged up shrubs and walls, scrambled over heathers and formed swags over arches. The display was magnificent.

Callum aided Ruby's attempts to take the very best photograph of their flamboyant colours, pointing out the best combinations and companions. He tied up wayward tendrils and removed any damaged leaf or faded bloom which might mar the perfect shot. It seemed cruelly ironic that he had time to garden now, but soon wouldn't have a garden in which to do it.

Amongst the clematis was honeysuckle climbing up in search of the light. A bit like Ruby and Callum in their search for a bright side. If they sold the house and bought somewhere cheaper, Callum's redundancy pay and Ruby's earnings would be enough to live on. She'd lose her precious garden, but that would happen no matter what they did now.

"We could still have a garden, Ruby, if we move away. You can work anywhere, can't you?"

"I can and if I'm to leave this garden I'd rather be somewhere I wouldn't keep passing it."

July

It seemed every Welsh roadside was set alight with the orange glow of montbretia. The flowers had to compete with the captivating views of mountains, rivers and valleys. Ruby would have been delighted with both had this just been a holiday.

"We could be happy here, Callum, don't you think?" If she said it with enough confidence, maybe it would be true.

"I think I could be happy anywhere with you, but yes, I do like it here." It took a while but they found the perfect place; built of slate and surrounded by a big expanse of green encircled with a low stone wall.

"I always wanted to live somewhere old, with character," Ruby admitted. They couldn't afford it in the city where Callum had worked. The house needed attention, but Callum would have time for that. The garden was all weeds and potential and fabulous views.

"I know they spread like crazy, but I think we should let a few of those montbretia stay in the garden."

"Me too. So we're doing it? Selling up and coming here?"

"We are."

At home the vibrant crocosmia, big blousy cousins of the delicate montbretia were in full flower. The plants were doing really well. If they were staying Ruby would have been getting ready to split the plants as soon as they were finished flowering. She'd have replanted some and still been left with spare pieces to give away. No, to take away. She'd divide them as planned and pot up a few clumps to take to Wales. Perhaps she needn't give up all her cherished plants.

August

From the fragrant pinks up to the imposing delphiniums, every plant seemed to be demanding attention and jostling for space. Not all of them were winning the struggle. A delicate, blue-edged white campanula was all but smothered and would have to be relocated if it was to survive, and a clump of silvery poppies were swamped by taller neighbours. The jasmine was covered in scented blossom, but it was also covering two rose bushes itself, threatening to overwhelm them. Despite all that, the garden was looking and smelling fabulous and taking a gorgeous photograph for the calendar wasn't at all difficult. It was a wrench to leave it to travel up to Wales and complete all the paperwork for purchasing their new home. It meant three days less in the garden she loved.

Ruby wasn't sure the trip was entirely necessary, but Callum was keeping himself busy by dealing with all the arrangements and determined to do things properly. She didn't have the heart to suggest a few phone calls and an email might do just as well. When she stepped out into what would become their new garden she was glad they'd made the journey. All that empty space, just waiting to be filled. This time she'd do things differently. Delicate treasures would go in a separate bed where they'd be able to compete on equal terms for space and water.

"I was thinking maybe we'd have room for a small pond," Callum said.

Ruby smiled. She wouldn't do things differently; they would. The new garden would be a team effort, both to create and to maintain. It would be better for that alone. She was eager to get back to the old one, so she could take cuttings, make divisions and collect seeds to start the new one.

September

The low sun lit up the hydrangea so it glowed as warmly pink as the sunset above it. Ruby thought the photograph of that might be the best she'd taken so far.

"Are you still going to make the calendar?" Callum asked.

"Yes. Why not?"

"I thought it might make you sad, to be reminded of what you'd left behind."

The thought of leaving did still sometimes make her sad, but she didn't think the photos, or memories they'd conjure, ever would. Ruby gestured to the pots she'd filled ready for the move. "We're not leaving it all and it'll be nice to look at while we're getting the new garden established. I've taken other pictures too, to remind me of mistakes I've made here, so I can avoid them next time."

"You really are OK with the move then? Not just putting

on a brave face?"

"I will be if you help me dig up the hydrangea. We'll need a dustbin sized pot, but I think it'll transplant OK."

It was strange to think that although they'd keep the bush, she'd not see it looking like this again. The acid soil in the new place meant the flowers would be blue next year. That would be just one of so many changes.

October

The dahlias were still flowering when Ruby and Callum cut them down and dug them up. They were taking them with them, so needed to get the tubers dried out. Callum gathered all the blooms into an enormous bouquet for Ruby to photograph. They looked so cheerful massed together like that, almost as cheerful as Callum. Lately he'd been reading up on oxygenating plants, sketching pond designs and researching the wildlife they might hope to attract.

As well as the dahlias, Ruby lifted sections of hosta. They'd look lovely round Callum's pond, especially if he encouraged enough frogs to keep down the slug population. The pinks and carnations they'd leave for the new owners who'd admired them. The plants wouldn't like the acid soil of the new garden and would wither away. Ruby would instead grow something that would flourish there just as she and Callum would. That yellow flowered azalea they'd seen once in a public garden perhaps. The scent had filled the air and she'd longed for one herself. Now she could have it.

November

The winter jasmine bloomed early as though not wanting them to miss it, or to remind them to take a piece with them.

They found a section already rooted and potted it up. A sharp frost that night meant Ruby was able to take a photograph of the yellow flowers in an icy coating. That seemed appropriate as the whole calendar was of a garden frozen in time.

December

The end of the year, and of their time in the old garden, was very cold and wet. In a way it was a blessing they were leaving with it looking so dull. It was easier to look forward to a fresh start in the New Year.

"What will you take for the last picture in the calendar? Callum asked. "It seems such a shame to end it this way as every other month looks so beautiful and optimistic. Those photos you did for me early in the year saved my sanity I think."

So he'd loved and appreciated her even when his misery had stopped him showing it. She was doubly glad then that she'd taken the pictures for him.

"It does seem a shame and I confess I considered buying a flowering Christmas rose to photograph, but that would be cheating."

"And it's not like we don't have enough pots of plants."

"True." As she turned to go back into the house she saw it. Their new garden in embryonic form. The collection of pots didn't look much she supposed, especially as many of the herbaceous things had died down and the cuttings were no more than twigs but to her it was full of promise. Looking at the pots, and the envelopes full of saved seed she could see the fun they'd have creating a brand new garden. She took a final photograph, the most hopeful of the twelve.

23. A Year In The New Garden

<u>January</u>

Whilst unpacking the last few boxes I come across the calender I made with photos taken in our previous garden last year. When I came up with the idea of making it, I didn't know we wouldn't be staying there. By 'it' I mean the calender, but of course the same thing applies so much more to the garden itself. We'd bought a big new house on a big new estate just after Callum's promotion to bank manager. So much has changed since then. That unpromising patch of churned mud became a garden. A gorgeous sun trap of a garden which I loved. Now we're in Wales and I don't think it'll ever stop raining.

Unsure if it will cheer or taunt me, I look at January's picture. It's of a patch of bright magenta cyclamen coum. I don't have a patch of them now, just a couple I potted up and brought with us. They're flowering, Callum tells me after he's dashed through the rain to put the rubbish bin out.

"That's something," I want to sound positive, but find myself adding, "They won't thrive here. I'll have to be careful where I site them just to keep them alive. Wales is wetter than our old home."

"There are rocks though and we could make raised beds to give them the good drainage they need. With a bit of care they should fit in here, just as we shall."

I'm surprised by his enthusiasm, but I shouldn't be. Of course this garden is his too. Further promotion to area manager for the bank meant I'd hardly seem him for a couple of years. That's exaggerating, but it's how it felt at times. My consolations were the garden and going freelance with my graphic design work, so I could spend time in it. Callum's sacrifice was rewarded with redundancy. We'll build a new garden together, just as we did before. I grab some paper and we begin sketching ideas.

"Maybe the cyclamen will spread just as they did back home. They might reach out and mingle with the local plants, flaunt themselves against the rocks," I suggest.

Before Callum can reply there's a knock at the door.

"I'm Mrs Davies," our visitor informs us. "Your nearest neighbour, so I thought I ought to welcome you to Llangollow."

We invite her in and offer tea. I don't apologise for the mess, she must realise we've not had time to get sorted out.

"That's not the right place for the fridge," we're told. "Mrs Jones had hers in that corner where it's cooler in summer."

"Milk and sugar?" I ask.

"It doesn't seem right to be sat here without the Jones's," she says. "Nice people, the Joneses. Everyone liked them."

"We didn't force them to sell!" I want to scream, but of course I don't. I won't be doing any flaunting or mingling myself much, not if Mrs Davies' attitude is anything to go by.

"We shouldn't be here, that's her opinion," I say to Callum once she's gone.

"She'll come round when she sees we're nice people too," Callum says. "Now how about a pond? I reckon they'll be enough rain to fill it."

"There's enough of that for a lake."

February

The calender image shows vibrant yellow aconites, the flowers contrasting with their own ruff of green leaves and the earliest purple crocus and snowdrops. We have a few of each still, blooming now in pots. We stand them where we think they'll look good and discover crowds of bulbs peeping through the surface.

"Are they snowdrops?" Callum asks.

"I think they might be. We'd better not disturb anything much until we know what's here."

The garden had been rather overgrown when we viewed the house, but clearly had been well tended at one time. Who knows what treasures might lie under our wet soil?

By mid month sheets of snowdrops burst into bloom. In a small space between patches we plant our own winter bloomers. They don't make a huge impact yet, but do add to the overall effect.

Mrs Davies arrives as we're almost finished. She's brought the church newsletter.

"The Joneses went to church every Sunday," she informs us. She doesn't stop for tea. "I can see you're busy."

Shame, you won't get to see we've not moved the fridge, I think.

March

Iris were the flowers I'd chosen to illustrate this month. We don't have any here. Instead, oh so appropriately, there are daffodils. Neat clumps of miniature ones near the house and a riot of larger daffodils along the far hedgerow. Huge golden trumpet kinds, more refined white petalled ones with deep orange centres, top-heavy doubles and slender stemmed multi-headed forms. I can't help but smile when I see them.

We're filling the bird table when Mrs Davies arrived. "The Joneses didn't feed the birds. They had a cat."

"We don't have any pets," I tell her as mildly as I can manage. "Would you like tea?"

She doesn't mention the fridge. I can feel her not mentioning it.

We decide to show our faces at church. I'm not religious, but Callum used to go to Sunday school and sang in a choir when he was a boy, and we were married in church. He'd gone occasionally afterwards, but not for some time. Here in Llangollow it seems the only social life revolves around the church or the pub.

Mrs Davies greets us almost warmly and introduces us to a few people before the service. Afterwards the congregation are invited to stay for coffee and I find myself chatting to a group which includes Mrs Davies and the lady who created the flower arrangements.

"They're beautiful," I say quite truthfully. "You've done a wonderful job."

"I do what I can, but it's difficult now I don't have much to work with."

It's true our little local shop only offers the spray carnations she's artfully placed amongst an array of greenery and daffodils but have to restrain myself from pointing out that, although bought flowers are scarce, there's plenty of material in gardens. Even if she's not lucky enough to have a garden herself, other church goers must do. I give a tactful hint by saying how well our daffodils contrast with the red dogwood stems and brilliant green new foliage on the willow.

At home I walk approvingly round our garden. As well as the daffodils we have an abundance of variegated foliage, coloured stems and shrubs about to burst their buds.

April

Colourful tulips shine out from the calender, almost like stained glass windows lit up by the sun. I've always loved tulips, we both have. That's part of the reason we had our honeymoon in The Netherlands. We bought tulip bulbs then and added to them every year until the display was truly magnificent. I felt that in a way they symbolised our marriage. The bulbs don't move well though and they don't like wet conditions, so we didn't bring many with us. They're blooming, but look a little lost.

Callum is at church again. I was surprised he wanted to go. He'd gone sometimes where we lived before, back when I was just getting going with freelance work and doing it alongside my regular job. That meant working weekends and I'd assumed his main motivation was to let me concentrate. He'd stopped going once pressures of his job left him with Sundays as his only free day. Again I'd made an assumption; that naturally he'd want to spend the entire time with me. Maybe I was wrong about that. He certainly doesn't mind leaving me at home now. Not just Sunday mornings either; he's joined the choir and attends practises.

Religion is a difference between us. It's not the only one; he seems to have lost his enthusiasm for the garden. He'd designed the pond and started digging, but when I suggested we measure up to see how much liner to buy he'd stopped. He's drawn up plans for a kitchen garden with raised beds too.

"I could build them and put in arches for runner beans and squashes. We could have a greenhouse too," he'd said.

I'd loved the idea, but now whenever I ask he just fobs me off.

May

Dicentra, the bleeding heart, is flower on the calender this month. It's as appropriate here as it was in the old place. Clearly the Joneses had loved the plant and it loves the conditions. As well as the piece I brought, there are established clumps of the same variety, pushing up through where the daffodil foliage is withering away. In other places there are white flowering versions and one with golden foliage.

This time last year Callum told me about his redundancy and with tears in his eyes he'd asked me to tell him he wasn't going to lose me too. I cry; at that memory, at the way Mrs Davies constantly compares us unfavourably with the Joneses, or rather me, Callum seems to be accepted. At the way my husband and I no longer feel like a team. We're together nearly all the time now, except when I'm shut away working or he's at church. Shouldn't we be drawing closer, not further apart?

"Ruby? What's wrong?" he asks me now.

I hadn't realised he was back from choir practice. Not knowing where to start, I mumble something pathetic about Mrs Davies not liking me.

"There's something you can do about that, if you really want to."

"Oh?"

"I found out the Joneses supplied most of the flowers to decorate the church. If you don't mind doing the same, I'm sure that would make a difference."

I remembered the conversation with the lady flower arranger. I thought I'd been so tactful, but must have given a very different impression.

"Oh yes, let's offer. We can easily spare some."

"Before you go out in the garden, could you give me a hand moving the fridge?"

"Oh?"

"We're going to have to put it where the Joneses did; that's the only spot where it won't have the sun on it at least part of the day." He looks apologetic.

June

The clematis is this month's calender flower. The few plants I brought with us are only just getting going, but the ones planted by the Joneses are an impressive sight. There are more than I'd had room for before. The same is true of scented shrubs. Callum and I cut great armfuls of viburnum, lilac, mock orange and roses for the church. There's such an abundance in the garden and I've realised cutting some will be a start towards the massive pruning job.

"These will smell even better inside than they do out here," he says as we get everything into buckets of water.

"I'll have to come on Sunday myself to see how they look and smell... and hear you sing too." That afterthought should have persuaded me to go before now.

"I'd like that." The warmth in his voice and the way he squeeze my hand show me the truth of that.

"How about I help you deliver this lot and stay to listen to you practise?"

He's pleased with the idea, I see.

So is Mrs Davies. "How generous of you, Mrs Mortimer. Look, Mary, Mrs Mortimer has brought you lots of flowers to arrange."

By the time we've got everything into the vestry and recut the stems to ensure they take up water properly we can hear the singers.

"Lovely voice your husband has," Mrs Davies says.

"Were Mr and Mrs Jones in the choir?" I can't help asking.

"That's right, yes," Mrs Davies says.

"He couldn't hold a note and she couldn't remember the words!" Mary informs me.

So, not quite perfect then. Neither are Callum and I of course, but we're good together. We must remind ourselves of that.

July

The montbretia is in flower again, just like it was the first time we saw this garden. Knowing it was staging a takeover bid, we'd dug up quite a lot. There's plenty left though, especially along the hedge. It flows around the boundary like a river of lava and helps blend the garden with the countryside beyond.

Actually plenty is an understatement. We still have too much, so I pot some up and take down to the church. They'll last longer like that than they would as cut flowers.

"Mrs Jones never did anything like that!" Mrs Davies says.

"If Mary would like to cut them then of course she can." I

speak through gritted teeth.

"Thank you, but I don't think I shall," Mary says. I'm starting to like her a lot.

When my ally mentions the local show and adds, "It's so important to keep these local traditions alive," I agree enthusiastically.

"So which classes will you be entering?" Mrs Davies asks. She then treats me to a detailed description of Mr and Mrs Jones's many triumphs with cookery and horticultural exhibits. Apparently there wasn't a single cup or trophy without their name on it at least twice.

August

I look at the towering delphiniums on the calender this month. We've decided not to grow them here; the strong winds make it impractical. Even the ones photographed in our previous, sheltered garden had needed support to keep them upright.

Callum has been wonderful. I have the time for both my paying work and the garden because he does every bit of the housework and takes care of my invoicing and accounts for me. He's helping us fit into Llangollow too by taking an active part in the church. Despite knowing he likes me there to hear him sing, I hardly ever go.

On Sunday I do. Both Mrs Davies and Mary greet me and remind others that the flowers come from my garden, which makes me feel less awkward about my infrequent attendance. The choir sings beautifully. I tell Callum so as we walk home hand in hand.

"I'm sorry; I should have come before to support you."

"It's all right, Ruby. I know going to church isn't your kind of thing."

"It isn't, but I could have gone sometimes, or to the coffee mornings or something. Like you with the garden, I know you're not really interested, but you work so hard to help me."

"Not interested? Why would you think that?"

"You didn't want to buy any pond liner, or work out the best site for the greenhouse …"

"Ruby… I… those things cost money and you're the only one earning any."

That's true, but when he'd been earning far more than me, the money was ours not his and we have enough still for those things. Eventually I get him to see sense.

"I think all this talk of the Joneses got to me," he says. "He worked in a bank too, but Mrs Jones stayed at home making cakes for the coffee mornings, jam for the WI, entering things in the village show. They're so well respected I started feeling inadequate and that their way of doing things must be right."

"It probably was for them, but we're not the Joneses, are we?"

"Perhaps I'll open the door to Mrs Davies in my pinny next time she comes, just to remind her of that?"

I half hope he's joking and half want to know how she'd react.

<u>September</u>

The hydrangea flowers on the calender are a warm pink, backlit by the sun. The ones in the garden are such a brilliant blue they more than make up for the lack of delphiniums and yet they come from the same plant. Digging it up had been quite a job but well worth it. As I'd predicted the difference in soil acidity has made a huge impact to the colour. Much as I liked it before, it's better now.

"Are you going to put it in the show?" Callum asks.

"I will if you enter your Victoria sandwich cake."

"Deal!"

We check the schedule to see there really is a class for both. There is and for all manner of other things too. Selections of vegetables are wanted, salad ones on a plate, others on a tray. Three stems of dahlia are called for and five stems of dahlia, a single specimen dahlia, ten mixed dahlia… and we have plenty of dahlias.

"Are you thinking what I'm thinking?" Callum asks.

"That we should put in as many things as we can?"

"We can't beat the Joneses on quality, but perhaps we can with quantity."

We grin at each other. Whatever else Mrs Davies might have to say she won't be able to say we haven't tried.

What Mrs Davies actually says is, "Congratulations!"

She says it as though she thinks her word is deserved, but I'm not sure why. Between us we've collected a bunch of highly commended cards, two third places and one second. We've won £1.40 which is less than half what we spent on entry fees at twenty pence a go. On the minus side we've had two exhibits rejected as 'not according to schedule'. Something I just know never happened to the Joneses.

"You've won the best newcomer cup," Mrs Davies tells me.

Naturally we're delighted and it seems as though she too is pleased.

October

Just like last year we gather the last of the dahlias, before the frost spoils them, and make a huge bouquet. The result is easily as good as the one featured on the calender. I place it in pride of place on the hall table, next to our trophy. The Llangollow show newcomer cup with 'Mr and Mrs Mortimer' engraved on it and no mention of anyone called Jones.

I give it another quick polish with my sleeve, even though I know Callum will keep it nice and shiny.

November

This month the calender shows a sprig of winter jasmine encased in ice. It's cold in this garden too, but elsewhere things are thawing. Mary the flower arranger calls me Ruby now and, although she doesn't expressly invite me to use it, Mrs Davies tells me her name is Blodwen.

December

I turn over the new page on the calender, almost expecting to see a Christmas rose. Instead I see the picture I'd taken of artfully arranged pots brimming with the plants ready to be brought here. They're all planted out now. One or two haven't survived, but on the whole everything has taken very well and the garden is well on the way to becoming a success.

"You will come to our Christmas party, Mrs Davies?" I ask when she calls round.

"If you are sure there will be room. You do seem to have invited a lot of people. I don't see how you'll accommodate them all in your lounge."

Mrs Jones had held small select little gatherings. Ours isn't going to be like that.

"We're having it in the kitchen and on the patio. Callum is putting up a huge tarpaulin in case it rains and we've got a couple of fire baskets. As well as providing heat we're going to roast chestnuts on them and heat the mulled wine."

"What fun that sounds! The Joneses never did anything like that. I would very much like to come… Ruby."

"We'll be delighted to see you, Blodwen."

The party is a huge success though I say so myself. Callum and his fellow choir members sing carols which everyone joins in with, even those who can sing no better than the Joneses. Actually including those who sing exactly like the Joneses: we invited them too.

24. Not Disappointing The Kids

I'd started to feel as though I'd become something of a disappointment to my kids. Although they loved me, I was in need of improvement.

"What about a book group?" June, my oldest, asked.

I gestured at the stack of holiday brochures April had left, and my seed catalogues. "I've got enough reading matter, thanks. Besides, I'm not really interested in what people think about girls who've gone, are on trains or have tattoos."

Glancing at the leaflet she'd brought, I saw I'd been half right. The book of the month was 'The Girl who Lied'.

"I know you all mean well suggesting these activities, but they're not my sort of thing. I've started digging a pond. After that, I don't feel like getting dressed up in the evening."

"How about a holiday once it's sorted out? The brochures are for interesting trips for singles."

"I can't go away in the spring as I have seedlings to tend and in summer there's the watering… I might consider it next winter."

Actually the trips seemed even less my sort of thing than the book group, walking group and evening classes my dear offspring seemed convinced I needed.

"We worry about you being on your own, Mum."

"Why? I'm perfectly happy, fit and healthy."

"Wouldn't you like to meet someone else?"

"I meet people all the time. Staff in the garden centre, the chap who services the lawnmower, passers by who stop to say how pretty the garden looks …"

"You know what I mean," June said.

I did and wasn't exactly against a spot of romance. "In theory, meeting the right man might be nice, I suppose."

"You need to make some effort then."

That's where I couldn't agree. To my mind, the right person wouldn't need me to make an effort as we'd have interests in common and accept each other as we were. If he thought I needed as much improvement as the kids clearly did, we wouldn't be suited.

June and her sisters brought me leaflets for dating sites and dances and other things which sounded awful. I forgot to do anything about them. There was something more important on my mind; the lawnmower wasn't cutting evenly. I called 'the chap' who services it. Actually Phil's a friend but if I'd explained that to June, she would… Actually I'm not sure how she'd have reacted, but it wouldn't have stopped her trying to fix my life when it was just my old mower which needed attention.

Phil got the blade levelled even before I'd brewed a pot of tea and sliced the walnut cake.

As we enjoyed our elevenses he told me about his rockery. "The most interesting plants are getting smothered. I think I need to dig it all up and start again."

"Maybe it's not as bad as you think," I said. "Shall I come round and take a look?"

"Please."

A few days later I remembered the promise and went round to Phil's place. I was surprised to see him dressed in a suit, until I remembered we hadn't actually set a time and date for my visit. Almost guiltily I realised 'six-thirty, Wednesday evening' stuck in my memory because it was the time for my children's latest attempt to sort me out.

"They booked me in for speed dating would you believe?" I said to Phil.

"Actually, I do. My own kids did the same to me. I'll cancel too and that'll leave the numbers even."

It didn't take Phil long to change, nor for me to see the rockery really did need a complete overhaul. We were soon potting up plants he wanted to keep and hauling out the stones to reach the roots of the plants which had taken over.

"Thanks so much for pushing me into it. I'd probably never have got round to tackling it otherwise," he said.

"Don't thank me yet, we haven't finished!"

It took a week of hard graft, but eventually the rockery was cleared of the unsuitable plants and reassembled with the rescued treasures and a few new introductions. Phil praised my energy and skill as he expressed his gratitude.

Having someone appreciate my good points was a refreshing change from the attitude of my children. Sometimes it was hard to remember I hadn't always been a disappointment to them. When they were little they were pleased to have two parents including a stay at home mum. Probably because it was very different from their friends' experience. My girls seemed to think that by being happy in my marriage and fortunate enough to, just, afford not to have to work full-time, I was somehow pushing boundaries.

I'd made ends meet by tending a huge allotment which provided more than enough vegetables for us all and working part-time in the supermarket once they started school.

My three said they were proud of me during my late husband's short illness and all that came after. When I gave up the allotment and joined a flower arranging group they were pleased I was being sensible, moving on, making friends.

The disappointment set in gradually. I went from cool earth mother to ordinary, middle-aged woman with a passion for gardening. To me it was new and exciting to grow plants for colour and scent rather than to fill bellies.

Although delighted I still saw my girls frequently, I didn't want them running my life. They thought they were being terribly subtle about it, but I realised the children's attempts, to solve problems I didn't have, were no longer random. They had something, and someone, definite in mind.

My attempts to avoid being set up with Mr Alright-by-them, were successful until April invited me round for dinner.

"I'd love to," I surprised her by saying.

I saw it as a good chance to really crack on with gardening tasks, as I wouldn't need to reserve time and energy to feed myself. She saw it as a matchmaking opportunity and was clearly very disappointed when I arrived too tired for witty conversation and smelling of compost.

Just as well I hadn't spent ages getting ready as the man they'd hoped to set me up with didn't arrive. Apparently he'd mixed up the date. I wondered what he'd have made of my scruffy top; probably a sigh of disappointment like my girls, rather than remarking it brought out the blue of my eyes as Phil had.

Summer did her best to get me to attend a barbecue one

Sunday afternoon. That didn't appeal. I've never been a fan of food that's raw in the middle, burned on the outside and smelling of firelighters all over.

"How thoughtful," I said, not letting on I knew that if I turned up I'd be introduced to the man my girls were conspiring for me to meet. "But on Sunday I'll be at Wisley gardens."

I then rushed round to see Phil and made the arrangements so my statement was true.

"I'll be your alibi," he said. "On the condition that you let me buy you lunch."

We had a lovely time looking at the alpine house, rose gardens and long borders. Conversation was easy, our cafe lunch perfectly cooked and we bought plants before we left.

Over the next couple of months I pretended not to notice what my offspring were up to and accidentally on purpose, sabotaged all their attempts. Phil was a great help.

"I've told my daughters a friend wanted to see me," I'd say when I arrived on his doorstep, rather than falling in with their plans.

"And so I do. Come in and I'll put the kettle on."

I suspect my kids were on to me fairly soon and enjoyed the game themselves. Why else would they continue trying to fix me up when it must have been obvious I wasn't sitting at home pining away from loneliness?

June got crafty. One day she rang to suggest a get-together with myself, her, April, Summer and all their partners and children.

"Everyone is free next Friday evening. How about you?" she asked.

I saw them separately quite often, but rarely all together

and the idea appealed so much I overlooked the likely ulterior motive and agreed.

"Excellent!" June said. "There's not really room in any of our houses, so we're going to the charity fancy dress party in the village hall. I'll pick you up, so you don't forget to go."

The Thursday before, I visited the beauty salon on the High Street. If you're thinking that doesn't sound like my sort of thing, you're right. April persuaded me to accompany her.

"I want a restyle, Mum, but I don't want them to talk me into anything too wild."

I fell for that and for having my nails done as there was a buy-one-get-one-free offer.

"They'll make you look glam for the party, Mum," my daughter said. Clearly she and her sisters were still up the their matchmaking tricks.

Not long after I'd got home, my neighbour came round about his hedge. It's one of those leylandii monstrosities. I'd requested it be trimmed, even offering to do the work myself.

He'd said, "I'll think about it."

That reminded me of all the times I'd promised my kids I'd think about sharing my life with someone else.

My neighbour obviously meant it, as that afternoon he said, "If you really want to get rid of the hedge you can. Has to be the whole lot mind."

"Oh! Right. I will then."

As soon as he'd gone, I phoned Phil with the good news.

"Let's do it now, before he changes his mind," Phil said.

Half an hour later he'd brought round his tools and we'd

started work. It was hard graft sawing, lugging and shredding. We worked until dark and started again first thing the next morning. We grabbed a quick sandwich at lunchtime and carried on. It's one of those jobs which looks worse before it looks better and I didn't want my neighbour to regret giving permission.

When June arrived, my hair suited the 'dragged through a hedge' description both literally and figuratively.

"Mum, there's blood on your face," she shrieked.

"That's probably just from rubbing my arm over it to get cobwebs out my eyes," I reassured her. There was no getting away from the fact I did have an impressive scratch on my arm.

"You look like a zombie!"

For a moment I was puzzled by her reaction. She's used to seeing me with chipped nails and foliage-stained, ragged clothes. Then I remembered she was picking me up for the party in the village hall.

"You did say it was fancy dress," I pointed out.

"Oh! I thought you'd spent the day gardening and were going to use that as an excuse not to go."

"Would I do that?" I asked sweetly.

"Yes, but you're not getting away with it this time."

After I'd greeted my family and been bought a drink, my daughters casually drifted towards a group containing the only other zombie there; Phil. Naturally after helping with the hedge he looked as bad as I did. Before either of us could say a word, one of his sons introduced us.

I gave Phil a wink and said I was pleased to meet him.

"Likewise," he said holding my hand a little longer than is usual in such situations.

Our various children began a clearly rehearsed conversation which revealed how much Phil and I had in common. Frankly it was a relief when they melted away and left us to talk.

"That didn't quite go to plan, did it?" he said.

"No. My ring looked so lovely after I'd had my nails done yesterday, that it felt wrong to show it off with my hands in the state they are now."

"I nearly said something, but my boys were so pleased to have got us together at last, I wanted them to enjoy the moment."

"Understandable. I hate disappointing mine too."

As we danced we came up with a new plan. Rather than Phil introduce our children to their soon to be step-siblings, we'd keep up the pretence of having just met. We're going to have a whirlwind romance and then give his boys and my girls all the credit for getting the two of us together.

Thank you for reading this book. I hope you enjoyed it. If you did, I'd really appreciate it if you could leave a short review on Amazon and/or Goodreads.

To learn more about my writing life, hear about new releases and get a free short story, sign up to my newsletter – https://mailchi.mp/677f65e1ee8f/sign-up or you can find the link on my website patsycollins.uk

More books by Patsy Collins

Novels –

Firestarter
Escape To The Country
A Year And A Day
Paint Me A Picture
Leave Nothing But Footprints
Acting Like A Killer

Non-fiction –

From Story Idea To Reader
(co-written with Rosemary J. Kind)

A Year Of Ideas:
365 sets of writing prompts and exercises

Short story collections –

Over The Garden Fence
Up The Garden Path
Through The Garden Gate

No Family Secrets
Can't Choose Your Family
Keep It In The Family
Family Feeling
Happy Families

All That Love Stuff
With Love And Kisses
Lots Of Love
Love Is The Answer

Slightly Spooky Stories I
Slightly Spooky Stories II
Slightly Spooky Stories III
Slightly Spooky Stories IV

Just A Job
Perfect Timing
A Way With Words
Dressed To Impress
Coffee & Cake
Not A Drop To Drink
Criminal Intent

Printed in Great Britain
by Amazon